For Eamonn

He opened the book, a new paperback, cracking the spine. His gaze moved rapidly down the page until he found the lines he was looking for. Keeping the place with his index finger, he flipped the postcard over and copied them out. As he did so, a memory surfaced: an afternoon in bed, snow falling outside, erasing everything but the warmth of her body, her smell, the touch of her mouth on his. When the ink was dry he wrote the name and address in the space provided, his hand shaking a little as the familiar characters shaped themselves, his thoughts occupied with an image of himself as he had been a year ago, in another place.

I

In the resonant quiet of the library, Saul's pen hung fire as a thought took shape. *Palimpsest.* He wrote the word at the top of his notes, then obliterated it with cross-hatching. Although it seemed an accurate enough description of his work in progress. He considered the pages of neatly handwritten notes and cross-references with vague contempt. To the traces of others' ideas, others' research, he had added his own scratchings, that was all. There was nothing original about it; originality, in fact, was not required. Everything that could be written or thought on the subject had been written and thought. His gaze fell on the open book:

> One day I wrote her name upon the strand,
> But came the waves and washed it away:
> Agayne I wrote it with a second hand,
> But came the tyde, and made my paynes his
> pray . . .

Agayne I wrote it with a second hand . . . Even Spenser had been there before him. Frowning, pinching the bridge of his nose between thumb and forefinger, he glanced through what he had written that morning, pausing occasionally to erase a word and substitute another.

Around him, on the mezzanine of the Reading Room, his fellow labourers in the salt-mines of the intellect bent over their books. From his position next to the brass rail which ran the length of the balcony and seemed designed to thwart the self-destructive impulses of its incumbents, he looked down on the balding or greying heads of readers on the lower floor. From time to time one of the heads rose and, propelled by its frail armature of muscle and bone, shuffled a few paces to the librarian's desk to submit a request slip. The only sound apart from the just audible flutter of turning pages was the compulsive coughing which moved around the room like a recurrent theme in a piece of chamber music.

Saul slipped the finished essay into its cardboard folder. It wasn't the best thing he'd ever done, but it was okay. And whatever he came up with, Richardson would find something to criticize. Screw Richardson. He pushed the folder away and began a letter to his wife.

> National Library
> Edinburgh
> 3 November 1976
>
> Baby,
> I miss you. The last few weeks have been a
> nightmare. Professor Richardson is a real bastard.
> Nothing I do for him is right. The food's terrible.
> And the rain . . . did I tell you about the rain?

As he wrote an image rose in his mind, like a photograph emerging from the developing tray, of the way she'd looked that time she'd seen him off at JFK. Already a month ago. Her face had worn a strained expression, the lips trembling, the eyebrows arched with the effort of holding back tears.

> The worst thing is, you're not here . . .

'Say, how about a coffee?'

Suppressing a groan, Saul looked up into the eager, red-bearded face of Robert Fischer. The things they had in common – both were studying sixteenth-century poetry; both were married, American and Jewish – did not in themselves, he felt, constitute grounds for a relationship. Robert evidently felt otherwise.

'I don't have time right now. I'm finishing a paper,' he lied.

2

Robert shrugged. 'Suit yourself. You going to the party tonight?'

'You mean that departmental thing? I guess so. Maybe.'

A man across the aisle made a fierce sound, as of escaping steam. Robert pulled a face, poked Saul in the ribs. 'See you there, okay?'

After this interruption, Saul found himself unable to resume his letter. *The worst thing is, you're not here.* Maybe he did need a break. He put the folder containing the letter and his essay on Spenser's *Amoretti* in his briefcase and went to get his coat. Descending the stairs he almost collided with a girl in black.

'Sorry.' Pale eyes flicked across his face.

They performed a little sidestepping dance, from which it seemed, for a moment, neither could break free.

'Sorry.' He saw her lips twitch with amusement as, grimacing, he made his escape.

In the street he felt himself engulfed by the cold air, the soft grey light of a November afternoon. He stood for a minute, uncertain which way to go. There was an hour to kill before his supervision with Richardson. He would have liked a cup of coffee, but was afraid of meeting Robert. Oh God. Robert. A nice guy. Undoubtedly a nice guy. So why did he feel like running a mile whenever he appeared? Perhaps it was no more than an automatic resistance to the assumption that, as expatriates, they ought to stick together. He decided to skip the coffee.

At the intersection he turned into a broad street of tall, crooked houses, once a mediaeval slum, now the preserve of antique shops and art galleries. His eye was struck by the irregularity of its buildings, the variegation of colour: pale stone, worn brick and painted plasterwork. It had charm, of course; maybe it was just perversity – a refusal to be easily seduced – which made him resistant to it. And to a mind accustomed to the logical grids of North American cities, there was something unsettling about the randomness with

3

which the place seemed to have been constructed. Here, along the volcanic ridge on which the Old Town had grown up, the architecture was Gothic, precipitous, fortress-like; below, the broad spacious streets of Georgian New Town offered a deceptively symmetrical version of the same confusion. Even with the tourist map he had bought on his arrival, he had more than once managed to lose himself, emerging, despite confident expectations to the contrary, in a strange part of the city, with all familiar landmarks lost to view.

In front of an archway whose spandrels were twin dragons, he paused to get his bearings. Castle, left. Cathedral, right. God, there were so many damn churches. At first he'd thought he could use their spires as points of navigation, but he found that, like the spires of Combray, they had a disconcerting habit of shifting their position when least expected. In the end he had given up trying to impose a system on his wanderings. It was only when you accepted the essential illogic of the place that the whole thing started to make sense.

> Yesterday I went to the castle. I guess you'd have
> enjoyed it. Maybe next spring we can go there
> together . . .

He'd lingered on the Esplanade in the rain, looking out over the black and grey city, its buildings as diminutive, from his vantage point, as those of an architect's model. In the distance, the antique silhouette of Calton Hill, with its unfinished temple, its ruined tower. *Jerusalem Athens Alexandria*, he'd thought, as the sun burst from behind a ragged cloud, illuminating the scene like a stage set. In that moment he'd felt himself entirely alone; an exile, like the eighteenth-century French prisoners of war whose cryptic messages defaced the walls of the dungeons he had visited that afternoon. It wasn't such a bad feeling. Cutting loose. Here, if he chose, he need no longer be defined by others' expectations;

4

could remake himself, in fact. It was a liberating thought; although not one he confided to his wife.

> Sightseeing's not much fun on your own. In fact, the more I see, the more I realize how much I miss having you there to see it with me . . .

Descending towards Canongate, turning his face from the sharp wind, he read the inscription on the wall of a ramshackle house, birthplace of the Calvinist zealot. LVFE GOD ABVFE AL AND YI NYCHTBOUR AS YI SELF. There seemed, to his mind, to be a contradiction between the generosity of the words and the dogmatic exclusivity of the system which had placed them there. On the pavement at his feet was a spattering of blood, the trace of some recent violence, each drop as round and distinct as a small coin. For a while he wandered, irresolute, glancing in the windows of shops selling items he had no intention of buying and at the faces of passers-by: people rushing in and out of restaurants and shops, or hurrying to keep appointments. Secret lives, thought Saul.

He bought a newspaper, stepping into a shop doorway out of the wind as he folded it open at the appropriate place. *Rooms To Let.* He scanned the column with a practised eye, noting with grim satisfaction that *Vegetarian, Non-Smoker* was still open to offers and that *Sunny Studio Flat, Morningside* hadn't yet been snapped up. As he took out his pen to circle the numbers – *Ring After Six* – his attention was caught by the adjacent window display, an arrangement of record sleeves featuring the leering white faces of the latest punk band. What a bunch of assholes. Of course, the name didn't mean a thing to him. He wasn't interested in street fashions. Especially not this one. In the dark glass he caught sight of his own reflection, its features distorted by a scowl. His clothes – flared jeans, slim-fitting jacket – struck him, suddenly, as out of style. Maybe he could use a haircut.

5

'Hey Saul . . .'

Crossing the street towards him came Magda Czyznski. With her long black cloak streaming behind her, her tousled hair streaked with grey falling around her shoulders, she resembled, Saul thought, some initiate of the Order of the Golden Dawn. Of all the people he had met since his arrival, she was the one he had warmed to most, despite – or perhaps because of – her raffish appearance, her clothes smelling of patchouli, her smoker's cough.

'So how's it going?' she said, as she caught up with him.

Another compatriot. Edinburgh was full of them. American Shakespeare scholars, American Joyce specialists, American devotees of D. H. Lawrence. It did nothing to mitigate his feelings of dislocation, giving him, rather, the sensation of having strayed into some colonial outpost of his native land, in which familiar structures had undergone a subtle metamorphosis.

'So, so.'

They began to walk back together, in the direction from which Saul had come, Magda setting the pace and doing most of the talking – a litany of complaints about the weather, the food, the deficiencies of British universities – in which Saul was able to join without much exertion.

'Did you find a room yet?'

'No.' He patted the folded newspaper in his pocket. 'I was just taking a look.'

'Still living with the dentist, eh?'

'You make it sound like we had something going . . .'

'With a good-looking guy like you anything's possible,' said Magda sardonically.

'Thanks, but Stuart's not my type. Are you going to this Eisenberg thing tonight?'

'Don't say it like that. It'll be great. He was Writer in Residence at Brown when I was there. Half the women were in love with him.'

'What about the other half?'

'You're just jealous.' They stood in front of the modernist façade of the National Library. 'Well,' she said, 'this is where I get off.'

'Guess I'll head on up to the university. Give Richardson another chance to rip me to shreds . . .'

'Have fun.'

Magda blew him a kiss and was lost to view within the glass blades of the revolving doors.

Displaying an unpredictability Saul was beginning to see as characteristic, Richardson was full of praise for his Spenser paper. At the end of his hour Saul left the glass and teak-veneer box of his supervisor's office with his faith in what he was doing restored. His research was of value; Richardson had said so and Richardson – for all his sarcastic humour – was the best in his field. As he traversed the broad expanse of the Meadows with its network of criss-crossing paths, he redrafted the letter to Virginia in his head, sustained, despite the cold and a sudden awareness that he had eaten nothing since breakfast, by his elated mood.

> Saw Richardson today. He seemed pretty pleased
> with my work so far. Coming from him, that
> means a lot . . .

He wondered if his wife would appreciate the significance of Richardson's approval. It was the kind of thing that could make a lot of difference when it came to getting a job. If Richardson would agree to write him a reference . . . Of course, it was stupid to build his hopes on one essay.

> Who knows? It might be useful when I start
> looking for university appointments in a couple of
> years . . .

And Virginia was the one who was so hot on finding him a job. She'd even tried to talk him out of Edinburgh, on the grounds that it would delay his chances of doing so another year. It had taken him a while to convince her that all the best appointments in his field went to guys who'd done at least a year of their research in Europe. And he had no intention of settling for anything but the best.

He bought himself a smoked cheese roll from the Italian shop on Melville and wolfed it down as he walked along. The consumption of food was one of several pleasures prohibited in his present accommodation. On the cracked chessboard path of a turn-of-the-century terraced house, he searched for his keys. Coat pocket. No. Trouser pocket. Damn. Briefcase. Aha.

The ground-floor room into which he let himself had been at one time, to judge from the items with which it was furnished – a clumsy deal sideboard, a standard lamp with a pleated parchment shade, an armchair upholstered with a design of molecular structures – the living room. It also contained Stuart's bed, the table on which he worked, the bookcase where he kept his medical books and the divan on which Saul himself had been sleeping. He was relieved to find his room-mate was out, if only because it meant there was space to turn around.

After showering – the word was not an accurate description of his ten minutes' naked shivering beneath a rusty trickle of water alternately scalding and icy – he ironed a shirt, then put on the dark suit he had worn for his graduation and, after a moment's hesitation, the tie Virginia had given him as a leaving present. As he combed his (slightly too long) hair, his eyes met those of his reflection in the cracked shaving-mirror. Their sombre glow betrayed his earlier euphoria. A man of potential, he told himself.

He met Stuart McLeish in the hall as he was going out.

'Hallo there.' Stuart's fairness was such that the slightest change of emotion suffused his freckled skin with colour. He's going to remind me about the money, Saul thought.

'Hi. Say, about that rent I owe you . . .'

'No bother,' said Stuart, holding up his hands. 'Give it us when you can.' His colour deepened. 'Ah . . . did I happen to mention that Linda would be staying this weekend?'

'As a matter of fact you did.'

'I mean, don't think I'm hassling you, but . . .'

'Hey, listen, I understand. Three's a crowd, right? Don't worry, I'll fix something. Leave it to me, okay?'

Conveying by his shrug a decisiveness he had not, so far, displayed, Saul edged out of the door and into the dark blue November night.

A little after seven he crossed the square in front of the university, which was surrounded on two sides by Georgian terraces and on the remaining sides by the concrete and glass monoliths with which, in the early seventies, it had been thought fit to replace them. He glanced up at the lighted windows on the ninth floor of the David Hume tower, his destination. Behind the locked gates of the park a man and a woman rearranged their clothing after an act of love. On the far side of the square the lights of the University Library were still burning. The air had a bitter, autumnal chill.

Arriving at the foot of the black granite and glass tower he waited for a few minutes for an elevator which seemed to have stopped between floors, then began to climb the stairs, two at a time. On the first landing he barely had to pause for breath. By the third his heart was beating strongly and he felt the blood moving rapidly in his veins. At the sixth he rested for a minute, leaning his forehead against the cold glass, his gaze moving across the darkened city with its network of lights, the broken reflection of a star in deep water.

Reaching the ninth floor, he removed his raincoat and folded it over his arm. He walked down the corridor until he came to a door, behind which the sounds of talk and laughter

9

could be heard. Smoothing his hair with the palm of his hand and squaring his shoulders in the narrow-waisted jacket of his new suit, Saul opened the door.

As he walked into the room he had the sensation of moving from silence and obscurity into a blaze of light. An explosion of faces. Someone was laughing loudly, a booming note above the general buzz of sound.

A voice said close to his ear. 'My God you *didn't* . . . What did he *say*?'

He looked round, startled to find himself addressed. The dark-haired girl who had spoken was looking at someone else however. A bearded guy in black.

'He didn't say anything. He wasn't too pleased though.'

'Silly old fool,' said the girl, dragging deeply on her cigarette.

Smiling apologetically, he edged his way between them towards the drinks table. He hung his coat on an overflowing rack and selected a drink from the array of little glasses already set out. The room was full, or almost full. Latecomers like himself were still arriving. *A desultory gathering of dons*, he thought, describing the scene for Virginia.

It was easier now than it had been on his arrival to distinguish members of the English faculty from research students, although there were confusing similarities. A fondness for the wearing of tweed jackets and corduroy pants was not in itself indicative of status. Several of his fellow postgraduates were indistinguishable from the dons in this respect, while a couple of the lecturers had adopted leather jackets and tight jeans as their preferred uniform. In America, academics dressed like the heads of corporate organizations. Saul wondered at the strange British capacity for blurring certain distinctions, while simultaneously creating new ones. He sipped his drink. Christ – what did it taste like? Distilled mothballs. If this was sherry, he must remember to avoid it in future.

Across the room, Richardson was talking to Leo Eisenberg.

The two men made an arresting couple. Tall, gaunt Richardson, with his shabby corduroy suit and his Nietzschean moustache, stooping a little to catch what the other was saying; short, powerfully-built Eisenberg, with his grizzled mane swept back over the collar of his velvet jacket, his saturnine actor's face, his booming laugh.

Everyone, Saul thought, had read at least one of Eisenberg's books. The Pulitzer prize-winning one about his childhood in New Jersey, or the one about his first marriage to the woman who'd ended up living with Lowell – or was it Schwartz? That was a great book. Although, on reflection, the last one he'd read, the one set in Budapest or Prague or someplace like that, hadn't been up to the standard of the early novels. There'd been a coarseness in the writing, a cynicism about his characters and about life in general which the writer had been unable to disguise. As if he were sick and tired of the whole performance.

Saw Eisenberg, Saul mentally scribbled in the margin of his wife's letter, *looking pretty good for an old guy. Wish I could say the same for his books. Maybe writing is like sex: the older you get, the harder it is to get it up . . .*

'Wasn't Leo great tonight?' Magda appeared from the crowd, exuding cigarette smoke. 'He really made the bastards sit up, didn't he?'

'Well, as a matter of fact – '

'I know, I know, you're going to say he's a reactionary old fart. He *is* a reactionary old fart. But you have to hand it to the guy, he knows what he's talking about. I mean, he has connections everywhere. Washington, the Pentagon . . .'

'I missed the lecture.'

Magda laughed. Barbaric chunks of hammered and twisted metal swung from her earlobes. Her wrists jangled with amulets and bracelets and her chain-smoker's hands (the index finger stained a deep yellow as if it had been dipped in dye up to the knuckle) glittered with rings in a variety of esoteric designs.

'You didn't miss anything new. The usual stuff about the death of the liberal humanist ideal. The new realism. Gillian, *hi*.' They were joined by the dark-haired girl in the tight velvet pants Saul had glimpsed on his arrival. 'So what did you think?'

'Hello, Magda,' the other said coolly. 'If you mean the, ah, talk, I thought it was quite good. Of course, it's not my period. Robin enjoyed it, though.'

'Oh yes,' agreed the tall, bearded guy in the black polo-neck. 'I thought some of the things he said about the failure of Modernism were quite, um, *provocative*.'

'The fact is,' Magda said amiably, 'there's no one to touch him. The guy's a genius.'

Gillian smiled unpleasantly, flicking away a fragment of ash from the front of her sweater. 'Oh, I wouldn't go that far,' she said.

'One has to admit,' Robin murmured, 'that last book of his was pretty awful.'

'It was a great book,' said Magda. 'Saul thinks it was a great book. Don't you, Saul?'

He was conscious of three pairs of eyes swivelling in his direction. The dark girl was frowning at him, her straight black brows drawn together in a way he found alluring. She had a pale skin, faintly marked with acne scars. A sullen mouth. He felt inclined to agree with her and her bearded boyfriend. The last book had been bad. But Magda was his friend.

He took refuge in prevarication. 'I, uh, certainly didn't feel it was the best thing he's done. But, uh, a writer of his calibre can get away with a bad book every once in a while.'

Magda frowned and shook her head, although whether at his judgement or at his betrayal of her he could not be sure. The slight movement was enough to set up a chain reaction of clashing earrings and bangles.

'Autobiography,' Gillian said with a triumphant sneer.

'Neither more nor less. Straight autobiography, with the names changed.'

'Bullshit,' said Magda pleasantly.

Saul noticed to his surprise that he had finished his drink. On the table beside the half-full tray of sherry glasses some bottles of wine had appeared. He edged away from the debate on Eisenberg's genius. As he stood looking for a clean glass, fragments of sound broke like waves around him.

'Whatever you say about Nixon, he was a professional. This guy's a complete jerk . . .'

The speaker was one of the American contingent, an irascible Chicagoan named Rakowicz, who was doing research into the novels of Thomas Love Peacock. It seemed incredible to Saul, for whom politics held little interest, that anyone could get so excited about the new incumbent of the White House. He found himself a glass and filled it with cheap red wine. As he extricated himself from the crush around the drinks table, the glass was almost swept from his hand by the gesticulation of a fierce-eyed Scot who was haranguing a small group of listeners on the iniquities of cultural imperialism.

'Look around,' he was saying angrily, 'and what do you see? Nothing but bloody Americans. And bloody English. All doing bloody English Literature.'

There was someone talking to Magda. A blonde girl in a red blouse, through which the outline of her small, high breasts was dimly visible. The horizontal creases of her tight skirt were like the pencillings of a nervous artist, suggesting the pelvic contours beneath. She glanced in his direction as he joined them, and he recognized the girl he had seen in the library that afternoon.

'He's married, of course,' Magda was saying, 'but they're kind of separated. Every time he talks about getting a divorce Muriel lays this guilt trip on him about the kids and the traumas he's putting them through.'

'It sounds messy.' The blonde girl lit a cigarette.

'It is. Sometimes I wonder why I got involved in the first

13

place. I mean, he keeps saying he's going to leave her, but then she has another of her breakdowns and – ' Magda broke off suddenly, noticing Saul.

'Don't let me interrupt,' he said.

'Catherine, this is Saul. He's from New York. Another expatriate,' Magda said, with what seemed to him a somewhat pained expression. Clearly she hadn't forgiven him his equivocation on the Eisenberg question.

'Hi.'

She returned his murmured greeting with a cool nod.

'Catherine gave a very good paper on the debate between Space and Time in the *Wake* and the parallels with Wyndham Lewis's *Time and Western Man* at the Joyce seminar last week,' Magda said, by way of a parting shot. They watched as she crossed the room to join the group around Eisenberg.

'Are you a Joyce scholar too?' Saul said, clearing his throat.

'God no. They're all Americans. It must be a national industry, don't you think?'

The faint condescension with which this was said filled him with resentment. In the same moment he realized how attractive she was. The mixture of sensations was confusing, like biting into a ripe peach and inadvertently lacerating your own tongue. He felt himself grow hot with annoyance and desire, of which annoyance was the greater part. Supercilious bitch. Sexy, supercilious bitch.

'I've no idea. I'm studying Spenser's allegory,' he said.

'That's a relief. I thought I might be in for an evening of intertextual parlour games. How many Dublin street names can you spot in the *Wake*. Name fifty species of insect in the fable of the Ondt and the Gracehoper.'

She smiled at him teasingly. Instantly he forgave her everything.

'You get a lot of that kind of thing in Spenser. Arcana, I mean. Numerology. Kind of like a Gothic cathedral. All these symbols relating to other symbols. The whole thing intelligible only to God. Or to the reader.'

14

'I hadn't realized Spenser was such a Modernist.' When she smiled, he caught a glimpse of white, slightly pointed teeth. The hand that held the cigarette was tipped with nails painted the same shade as her blouse.

'So are you a big fan of Eisenberg's, or what?' He was conscious of sounding aggressive. Well, what of it? He felt aggressive. All these people, with their pretentious talk, had soured his earlier mood.

'Do you mean the man or his novels?' She seemed unperturbed by his deliberate discourtesy; seemed rather, in fact, to have expected it.

'The books, I guess.'

'I like some of them. The early ones. His later stuff just seems like a projection of his public persona.'

It was what Saul thought himself. But for some reason he allowed himself to feel aggrieved on Eisenberg's behalf. 'That's unfair, surely? The guy can't help being a star. Why do you think he got asked to this little *festspiel* in the first place? Because he's a famous writer. A famous American writer.'

'That's just what I don't like about his books,' she said, with the faint note of condescension he had detected earlier. 'They've got Famous American Writer stamped all over them. Or right through them, like a stick of rock. If you know what that is.'

'*Brighton Rock*. Sure I do,' he said, affronted. 'I studied Greene in high school.'

'Poor you.'

He was aware that he was being mocked and was unsure how to counter it. There was a moment's silence. Her glass, he saw, was empty.

'Can I get you another drink?' he said.

As he entered the vortices of the crowd, he saw Eisenberg talking to the girl in velvet pants who'd hated his books. They seemed to be getting on fine. Reaching the bar, he refilled Catherine's glass and his own and made his way back towards the centre of the room where he had left her. He saw, with a flash of annoyance, that she was talking to the bearded guy.

'How's the book going, Robin?'

'Slowly.' He looked pained. 'You know how it is . . .'

'What's it called again? Bleeding Hearts or something . . .'

'*Open Wounds*. It was meant to be out in September but there've been some problems with the printers. Apparently the publisher hasn't paid its bills for ages and they're refusing to go ahead with the book until it's all been settled. It's very aggravating.'

'Tedious for you.' She glanced at Saul, by way of thanks, as she took the glass of wine. Again, he felt a slight but unmistakeable *frisson* of desire.

'I sent a proof copy to Flynn.' Robin looked distractedly around s he spoke. 'I was hoping he might do a preface. Just a paragraph or two, you know, on the new wave in poetry.'

'So what kind of poetry do you write?' Saul said, irritated by the guy's languid gestures, his air of world-weariness.

'It's, ah, hard to say exactly. How does one characterize one's own work, after all? I suppose you could say they were, ah, geometric exercises. Approximations.'

'I'd be interested to read them sometime. I used to write poetry myself. It's a phase you go through, I guess,' Saul said, with what he hoped was a veiled contempt.

'Possibly.' Robin's tone was icy. In the momentary silence, Leo Eisenberg could be heard telling an anecdote about John Updike. 'If you'll, um, excuse me, I ought to have a word with old Hobson,' Robin said, catching sight of the bulky figure of the Professor of Modern Literature. 'Gilly thinks he might be able to get us some part-time supervision work. She thinks it'll look good on the CV when we start looking for jobs in a year or so. Talk to you later, Catherine.'

'You were a little cruel, I thought.' Catherine smiled at Saul. 'He writes very nice poetry as a matter of fact.'

'I couldn't care less what kind of poetry he writes. I just

wanted to get rid of him,' he said with a sensation of recklessness.

She looked at him. 'Do I know you from somewhere?'

'The steps of the National Library. We almost ran into each other.'

She held his gaze for a moment. 'What brings you to Edinburgh? Apart from Spenser's allegory.'

'Oh, you know . . .' Out of the corner of his eye he saw his adversary, the poet, conferring with his girl. Both glanced in his direction. He grinned. 'Great climate. Terrific people. How about you?'

'It was the only place that would take me.' She scanned the crowd with an expression of boredom. 'It was either this or get a job.' It was impossible to tell from her tone whether she was joking or not. That was the trouble with the British, Saul thought.

'I know what you mean,' he said, thinking fleetingly of his wife, his commitments.

'Where are you staying?'

'Do you know Bruntsfield? I'm rooming with a guy from the School of Dentistry. It's kind of a temporary arrangement. I guess you don't know of any rooms for rent, not too far from the centre? I'm willing to pay extra for running water and an inside bathroom.'

'I might know of something,' she said with a shrug. Her eyes, he saw, had flecks of lighter colour around the central whorl of the iris. Smoke-coloured eyes.

'Say, Catherine, come and meet Leo, won't you?' Magda appeared out of the crowd. 'He says he didn't fly three thousand miles to talk to a bunch of Americans. So I told him we had some people here from Cambridge, England.'

'Thanks a lot, Magda,' said Catherine, making a wry face. She looked at Saul. 'See you later perhaps.'

'Sure.'

He watched her cross the room, her slender figure, elongated by the narrow skirt and high heels, appearing like some fabulous sea-creature, mermaid or nymph, amongst the drab shoals of academics. Grizzled Leo Eisenberg seized her hand as Magda introduced them and held it between his as if about to read her fortune. Saul thought, momentarily, about joining them. Maybe he should tell Eisenberg his latest book was crap. Instead, he went over to the drinks table and poured himself another glass of sour red wine.

'Ah, Meyer, there you are.' It was Richardson, beaming mildly at him from behind his bifocals. 'Enjoying the party?'

'Sure.'

'That's the ticket. Quite a good turnout, don't you think? Of course, Leo's always good value. Amusing fellow.'

There was an element of derision in the remark, Saul felt, a suggestion that being amusing was all Leo Eisenberg – an American, after all – was good for. Maybe, he thought, it was just another facet of the language problem. The famous British irony. A sort of cultural freemasonry by which the initiate could subtly mock the uninitiate. He made a non-committal sound.

Across the room, Eisenberg said something to Catherine which made her laugh. Richardson followed the direction of his gaze and said drily, 'Very amusing.'

'Yes.' Saul's grin felt frozen in place. He cast about for a suitable topic of conversation. His *Amoretti* paper. *Fayre eyes, the myrrour of my mazed hart*. He wondered whether Richardson, with his dry laugh, his ironic look, had ever been in love. Unlikely. 'What did you think of his last book?' he said.

Richardson raised an eyebrow. 'One doesn't have to *read* Leo to appreciate him,' he murmured. His attention was momentarily diverted. 'Excuse me, Meyer, there's someone I ought to . . .'

'Go ahead.'

Saul edged closer to the group around Eisenberg. From what he hoped was an unobtrusive position he gave himself up to looking at Catherine. Her gestures, her smile. *Fayre eyes*. From time to time as the buzz of conversation around him subsided, he caught a fragment of Eisenberg's talk, delivered in his sonorous actor's voice.

'Death,' he was saying, 'all my books are about death.'

'Oh, but surely . . .' An intense young woman in black twisted the stem of her wine glass as if about to snap it in two. 'A recurrent theme in your work is the nature of love . . .'

'Love and death, if you like,' Eisenberg agreed with a shrug. 'After all, it's the same thing. What does Mann say? *Le corps, l'amour, la mort, ces trois ne font qu'un.* I always meant to use that in one of my books, somewhere. Maybe the next one, who knows?'

'What's the problem, Saul? You're looking depressed.'

'Oh, hi Robert.'

'Pressure of work getting to you?' Robert said sympathetically.

'Kind of . . .' Robert was blocking his view of Eisenberg's acolytes. All that was visible of Catherine was the outline of her shoulder in its red blouse, the curve of her hip.

Robert nodded eagerly. There was nothing he liked better than talking about work. 'I did an all-night session a week or so back. The lecturer for Renaissance Poetry was sick so they asked me to prepare a paper on the Elizabethan love lyric to fill in. Went down pretty well.'

'Terrific.' Saul shifted his position in time to see Eisenberg murmur something in Catherine's ear. Love and death, he thought scornfully. Horny old bastard.

'Carol and I were saying,' Robert's nasal drone broke into his consciousness once more, 'you really should come to dinner one night.'

'I . . . That would be . . .' Saul cast around for reasons why this would not be possible and found none. 'It's a really nice idea, but . . .'

Eisenberg was on the point of leaving. Escorted by gaunt Richardson on the one hand and squat Hobson on the other, he made a leisurely progress across the room towards the door, stopping to talk to any woman who struck his fancy.

'Did you find a place yet?' said Robert. 'Because the offer's still open, if you want to crash at our place for a week or two.'

'Why thanks,' said Saul, 'I'll keep it in mind.' He felt a touch on his shoulder. It was Catherine, in the black, full-skirted coat she had been wearing when he'd seen her for the first time.

'Shall we go?' she said.

'Right away.' He threw an apologetic look in Robert's direction, 'See you around, Robert,' and moved away before the other had a chance to name a date and time. Catherine began to push her way through the crowd that had gathered around the door, as people collected coats and briefcases and exchanged valedictory remarks.

Saul caught up with her. 'You saved my life back there,' he said.

'Really? It was unintentional. I just thought you might like to have a look at the room. You did say you were looking for a room?'

'You mean now?'

'Why not? Unless you've got other plans, of course.'

'Isn't it a little late?'

'Oh, Liz and Guy won't mind. They're the people I live with. Liz was saying only the other day she wanted to get someone for the spare room. To help with the rent. Liz worries a lot about money.' The door closed behind them, shutting out the sound of voices. They stood face to face in the dark corridor. 'But if you'd rather come some other time, that's all right . . .'

'Oh no,' he said quickly. 'Tonight would be fine.'

On the stairs they passed Magda in conversation with the red-haired Glaswegian Saul had noticed earlier. 'It's a creeping menace,' he was saying loudly. 'All the more insidious because it's invisible . . .'

'Okay, okay, you've convinced me.' Magda acknowledged Saul's greeting with a faint grimace. 'You don't have to convince the whole building.'

'I mean, take the Scots . . .'

'Take the Scots. Take the Irish. Take the whole damn lot . . .'

'You're talking about an oppressed people. A subject race . . .'

'Who *is* that?' Saul said. 'Is he a student?'

'Who, Donald? God no, I shouldn't think so. He must be at least forty, wouldn't you say? I don't know what he does for a living. Probably nothing. Magda met him in a station buffet on her way back from Dublin. She spent a week there, following in the footsteps of Leopold Bloom.'

'Sounds like fun.'

'I believe it involved a good deal of drinking. Magda was keen to experience the authentic atmosphere of Dublin in 1904.'

'I could use a little authentic atmosphere myself right now.'

'It can be arranged.'

They crossed the dark square, skirting the railings of the park. The air was cold, with a smell of frost. Beneath their feet the stones rang like iron. In the blue-black sky the stars were cold points of light. As they reached the junction of Lawnmarket and George IV Bridge Street she touched his arm, barely grazing the sleeve. He jumped as if a live current had earthed itself along the nerves and tendons of his body.

'This is the quickest way back,' she said. 'Or we can go down Cockburn Street. There's a pub along there that isn't bad.'

'Let's go the slowest way, by all means,' he said.

A cold wind tasting of salt stung their faces as they turned into the gallows-haunted street, its blackened tumbledown tenements and broken paving stones giving it the look of an etching printed with too much ink.

'So what did Eisenberg have to say?' They were descending the worn steps into Fleshmarket Close. 'You seemed to be enjoying it.'

She laughed. 'He told me I had the face of a depraved

21

Madonna, whatever that means. He wants me to visit him in New York.'

'Will you?'

'I shouldn't think so. Not unless he pays my fare.'

Halfway down the narrow passage, scarcely wide enough for two people to pass in comfort, was the pub, its entrance set at an oblique angle to the alley. Inside was a smoke-filled parlour, walled with mirrors.

'What do you want?' She stood at the bar, tapping her foot on the brass rail.

'Whisky, I guess. No, give me some of that beer they have here. Bitter, or some name like that.'

'What do you make of the English department?' she said, as they waited for the drinks to arrive. There was nowhere to sit down. The few small tables, whose cast-iron bases were bare-breasted caryatids, were occupied. The atmosphere's dense nicotine haze was pierced by blasts of cold night air every time the door opened.

'It's okay,' he said warily. 'I mean, Richardson's good. He's the main reason I applied here, as a matter of fact.' Catherine watched as he took a sip of his drink, winced and set the glass down on the counter.

'Not much improvement on the wine, is it?' she said. 'You should have stuck to whisky.'

'It's not so bad. Really.' He managed another mouthful. 'It just takes some getting used to. I was thinking about your question. The thing is, everything's so unstructured here, after NYU. I don't know where I fit in, or if I fit in.'

'Everyone feels like that.' She lit a cigarette.

'Do they? I'm not so sure. What about Magda? She knows what she's doing, all right. Or your friend, whatshisname, the poet . . .'

'You really took a dislike to poor Robin, didn't you?'

'He was just so damned superior. *Approximations* . . . Christ!'

'Robin's a very nice person.'

22

'He's got a good-looking wife. A little hard to take, maybe . . .' In the mirror he caught the flash of malicious amusement on her face.

She met his eyes in the glass. 'I suspect you find us all a bit hard to take.'

'That's not true, believe me.' He signalled to the barman. 'Whisky, with ice. The same again for my friend here.' The clouded mirror threw back an image of her blonde head next to his dark one. They made a handsome couple, he thought. 'I have no right to criticize people I hardly know.'

'Why not? Superficial impressions are always the most accurate, don't you think?'

'Oh, sure.'

The drinks arrived. He sipped his whisky thoughtfully. For a minute he saw himself as if from a distance. A good-looking young man in a new suit, sitting with a girl in a bar in a foreign city. Really, things were not so bad. The whisky slipped down his throat like a tongue of fire.

'Tell me about these people I'm going to meet tonight,' he said after a short silence, during which he made a pretence of studying the other occupants of the bar. From time to time he stole glances at his companion. Her averted face – 'depraved Madonna' was good, he thought – was partly concealed by the gleaming fall of hair. Her red lips left a faint image of themselves on the rim of her glass.

'Liz and Guy? They're nice people. That's to say, I hardly know them.'

'Are they graduate students too?'

'They both work. Liz teaches. Guy's an architect. He's still doing exams, I think. I don't see much of them. It's the perfect arrangement.'

'Are they married, or what?'

'I think so.' She stifled a yawn. 'They're trying to have a baby. Liz keeps going for check-ups to see if everything's okay. At the moment they think it's Guy's sperm-count that's to blame.'

'Poor guy.'

'I suppose it is unfortunate, if you want kids. Although I imagine sterility has its compensations. No more messing about with inter-uterine devices and bits of rubber.'

Saul blushed. 'Another drink?' he said.

'God no. I've had enough. There's some whisky back at the flat if you want it. Shall we go?'

⁂

They descended the slippery steps into the vaulted reaches of Market Street. High above them the traffic whirred and shrieked over North Bridge. On Waverley Bridge images of the night city converged. Below them, the arterial branching of tracks, the subterranean roar of trains arriving and departing. Looking east, the slender columns of the pseudo-Parthenon. Westward, the squat fortress on its rock. In Princes Street crowds were laughing and shouting. Lighted shop windows displayed claymores, tartans. Bald, dismembered mannequins, their torsos chastely swathed in sacking.

As they walked down Dublin Street Saul had the sensation that the houses were rearing up on either side, their dark shapes threatening to overwhelm the puny figures in their midst. Tall tenements with lighted windows loomed like cliffs of stone. They reached London Street.

Halfway along a terrace of large stone houses, once fine, now a shade dilapidated, Catherine paused in front of a door from whose fanlight the glass was missing. 'This is it.'

The stairwell was poorly lit. He heard her miss her footing on the first-floor landing and put out a hand to save her, but encountered only air. She fumbled for a moment with her keys and there was the sound of a lock sliding back. He followed her inside, conscious as he stood there in the darkness of an expansion in the volume of space above his head. She snapped on the light and he stood in a large hall with doors opening off it on three sides. A large gilt-framed mirror reflected what light there was from the street door. On a high shelf a carved stone head of some classical deity –

Hermes? Dionysus? – stared down at the intruders with blind disdain.

She moved ahead of him, flicking switches. 'They must be out. Christ, it's cold in here.'

She flung open the door of a large room, lit only by a swathe of light from the hall and the colder illumination of street-lamps outside its two tall windows. There was the sound of a struck match as she lit the gas-fire. Its blue flames shot up and huge shadows reared on the ceiling. He saw a gleam of scales, a coiled and massive shape emerging out of the dark.

'Jesus, what's *that?*'

He found himself shuddering, not entirely from the cold.

'That's the snake. It lives here.'

She was laughing. He heard the soft rasping of her indrawn breath. Then she moved past him to switch on the lights. In the sudden glare the thing in the glass case looked smaller than he had at first thought it, its dusty coils absurdly posed in a simulacrum of menace. On the twisted branch which formed the substructure of the arrangement feathery bodies – jays, kingfishers, tanagers, hummingbirds, orioles, wrens – were poised within striking distance of the serpent's head. Tropical species clustered next to native woodland birds without regard for verisimilitude: bowerbirds consorted with magpies, drab finches wore the borrowed plumes of bee-eaters, starlings those of the painted halcyon.

'You see, it's quite harmless.' Her long white throat rippled with laughter.

'It depends what you mean by harmless.' He stared at the thing behind the glass, masterpiece of the taxidermist's art. In the electric light it seemed almost pathetic, ridiculously unstable, the heavy case balanced on barley-sugar legs which trembled with each slight movement, thin Victorian glass shivering beneath his touch. 'Why would anyone want a thing like that in their house?'

'I rather like it.'

'It suits the room, I guess.' He felt his display of nervousness had lost him some subtle advantage. 'Nice place. How did you find it?'

'Oh, you know, a friend of a friend.' She handed him a glass of whisky. 'Aren't you going to sit down?'

'Oh. Sure.' He perched uneasily on the edge of the sofa, shifting his glass from hand to hand. Despite the room's icy temperature he found he was sweating. Behind him, just out of his range of vision, Catherine crouched over the record player, like a young witch putting the finishing touches to some complicated piece of sorcery.

'Have you lived here long?' His voice cracked with the effort of trying to sound relaxed.

'A couple of months. Since the beginning of term in fact.'

The shimmering cadences of the overture from *Die Zauberflöte* drowned his next remark.

'What did you say?' She sat down next to him, crossing her legs with a whisper of nylon against nylon.

My God, he thought, I'm a married man.

'I said, you seem to know the place pretty well.' He gulped his whisky without thinking. In the lamplight her hair was a gleaming web of tiny filaments.

> *Zu Hilfe! Zu Hilfe! sonst bin ich verloren!*
> *der listigen Schlange zum Opfer erkoren!*

She smiled at him. It was the way he had seen her look at Eisenberg. A teasing look. He found his glass was almost empty.

'I like it here. I can't think how I ever lived anywhere else,' she said.

> *Barmherzige Götter! Schon nähet sie sich!*
> *Ach! rettet mich, ach! schützet mich!*

26

'Really?' His voice seemed to him a strangulated squeak. 'Don't you find it depressing? Nothing but grey stone houses. And those terrible churches. Like rockets on a launch pad. And the rain.'

'I agree it's something of an acquired taste. But I've never found it depressing.' She yawned, stretching her arms above her head.

He caught a whiff of sweat and perfume. Warm skin. Oh God. 'I guess it's okay if you like rain.' He was tense with the effort of talking about the weather. Christ. What would they talk about next? Maybe he should ask her what books she liked. 'Nice room,' he said.

In the light of the single lamp the room's proportions seemed exaggerated, the ceiling impossibly high, the floor space improbably wide. Or maybe it was the effect of the whisky. He noticed his glass was now full. The impression of austerity achieved by painted panelling, high windows and ornamental plasterwork was softened by the faded romanticism of the room's furnishings. The walls were papered with a design depicting birds of paradise in an enchanted forest. Lyre birds and parrots flew screeching through imaginary groves. Everywhere you looked there were birds, perching in the heavy folds of curtains and on the backs of armchairs. Their colours – pale orange, dull rose, verdigris, cobalt – were picked up in the worn threads of the carpet and reflected in the mirror over the fireplace, which threw back its warped images as if from the depths of a forest pool.

Catherine did not reply. He found himself intensely aware of her physical presence: the slight shifting of her weight on the sofa next to him, the movement of her hand as she brushed a strand of hair away from her face. The Queen of the Night began her aria. He closed his eyes, ravished by the voice's sinister beauty, its swooping coloratura. When he opened them again, she was bending over him.

'I thought you'd fallen asleep.'

With a feeling of recklessness he pulled her to him, knocking the rest of his drink onto the carpet.

'It doesn't matter,' she murmured, but whether it was the accident or the embrace to which she was referring he could not be sure. When they kissed her body twisted in his arms like a large fish, a mermaid. Strands of her seaweed hair fell across his face, her wet mouth tasted of salt.

'God, I feel drunk,' she said pleasantly, pulling away from him. 'I'd better show you the room.'

He stared at her. 'Oh, the room.' He got up unsteadily. Under the cold eye of the grinning snake, they swayed together on the threshold.

2

Saul woke in a strange room. Sun coming in through badly drawn flowered curtains. Walls papered with a blue and green trelliswork pattern, so that the effect was that of a painted cage. Bars of oily light lay across every surface, hugely magnifying the grains of dust. He lay for a while, watching their glitter and shift. The woman beside him on the bed stirred and flung out an arm across his chest. He remembered where he was. The trellis shimmered like the walls of an aquarium as he tried to sit up and fell back again with a groan. His companion muttered something.

'What?'

'I said, I'll make some coffee. Christ, I feel awful. How about you?'

'Not so good.'

On the dressing-table amongst a clutter of dusty jars and bottles something sparkled in the light. Broken glass. There was a powerful smell of expensive scent. She propped herself on one elbow, watching him. 'You broke it, remember? Last night.'

'I don't remember a lot about last night.' Try as he might, he could recall nothing beyond the point at which they had arrived back at the apartment. The snake. He remembered the snake. Jesus. His head hurt.

'It wasn't *that* bad,' she said, giving him an ironic look.

She sat up and swung her legs out of bed. Her body was white, slender, small-breasted, like Cranach's Eve. She stretched, yawned and, lithe as a dancer, stooped to retrieve her dropped robe from the floor.

When he opened his eyes the room was empty. Disconnected images drifted across his consciousness like spots across the retina. Torn between misery and desire he lay, shuffling the worn pack of last night's episodes – the party, the pub, the room and, somehow, her bed – until his head swam. She returned carrying two mugs of coffee, which she set down on the floor. She bent and kissed him, her mouth tasting of last night's cigarettes and a faint, ammoniac after-taste of semen.

'Liz and Guy are up.' She disentangled herself from his embrace. 'You'd better come and meet them.'

'You mean *now*?' He could not keep the alarm out of his voice. She did not reply but began hunting through the rubble on the dressing-table for something, a comb or a mascara wand.

'Oh fuck,' she said. 'Look.' She held out her hand for his inspection. A splinter of glass had pierced the tip of one finger, which was beaded with blood. She stared at it for a minute with what seemed to him unnecessary fascination. Then, holding her wounded hand in front of her, she began to comb her hair with short, fierce strokes.

Winter sunlight streamed with cruel brilliance into the kitchen, which was built on the same scale as the rest of the apartment, with a flagstone floor and what looked like pre-war fittings: vast cupboards, a stone sink, a cast-iron stove. It was here that the Urquharts received him, with a cordiality that seemed, in his present state of mind, almost excessive.

'Hello, Saul.' Liz smiled at him. 'Have some coffee. Help yourself to toast.'

'Help yourself to whatever you want.' Guy glanced up briefly from the newspaper he was reading. 'Interesting times in America,' he said.

'I guess so,' said Saul uncertainly, showering crumbs across the table as he attempted to butter a piece of brittle toast. In his now rumpled blue suit he must look, he thought, as disreputable as he felt. Shifty-eyed, unshaven. The remorseful adulterer. Oh, Christ, what had he done?

'Of course,' Guy's smile was self-deprecatory, 'you must be far better informed about the political scene there than I could ever hope to be . . .'

'Oh no,' said Saul. 'Not at all.' He wasn't even sure what day it was. Friday? No, Saturday. Had he said he'd call Virginia tonight, or was she supposed to call him?

'Although I try to keep up with developments.' Comfortable in his old brown dressing-gown, Guy tapped his newspaper. 'We ought to have a chat about it sometime.'

'Sure.' The toast and its accompaniment of bitter black coffee had added a new dimension to his hangover. He looked at Catherine. Had they talked before they'd fallen into bed? Had he, perhaps, told her about Virginia? He had no recollection of it. But then, he had no recollection of anything. Oh God.

'I should think Saul wants to talk about the room first, darling.' Liz beamed at him. In her high-necked, long-sleeved nightgown, her hair tied up in an intricate arrangement of curling-rags, she looked, Saul thought, like an Early American settler's wife. 'Catherine tells me,' she said to him, 'that you'd be interested in taking over the spare room.'

He nodded, glancing uneasily at Catherine.

'You looked at it last night, remember?' she said, with an expression of sardonic amusement. He wondered how she managed to remain so cool. His own self-possession was rapidly disintegrating.

'Oh, sure.' A vague memory of exposed floorboards, curtainless windows, an echoing space surfaced. 'It's a very nice room,' he said.

'It's a wee bit bare at the moment, but I'm sure we can find you a carpet and a few more sticks of furniture,' Liz said. 'At the moment there's just the bed.'

'And the wardrobe,' said Guy.

'And the wardrobe. But we wouldn't expect you to pay your full share of the rent. At least, not until we get it properly furnished.' She named a figure. 'Does that seem too much? It's inclusive of water but not gas or electricity . . .'

'It sounds fine,' said Saul. 'Would a monthly cheque be okay or do you want cash?'

'Oh, a cheque I think, don't you, darling?' Liz looked at Guy, who nodded. 'That's settled *that*, thank goodness. I hate talking about money, don't you?'

'Is it okay if I move in right away? Only I said I'd be out of Warrender Park Road by the weekend.'

'Move in as soon as you like.' Liz spread marmalade on a slice of toast and passed it to Guy, who chewed it with an abstracted expression as, business concluded, he turned to the crossword. 'It'll be nice to have another man around the place. Company for Guy. I think he gets a bit fed up with women's talk, don't you, darling?'

'I like women's talk,' said Saul.

'Do you really? I suppose that's because you're American. Have some more toast.'

'I think I'd prefer a couple of aspirin.'

'You poor thing.' Liz clicked her tongue sympathetically.

'It's nothing. I guess I'm not used to your British beer. Or your Scottish whisky.'

'It's my bad influence,' said Catherine.

An hour later Saul and Catherine walked up Inverleith Road towards the Royal Botanical Gardens. In spite of the aspirin he had taken, Saul's headache was worse. The winter sunlight glancing off the windscreens of parked cars struck him between the eyes with almost palpable force. Worse than the headache was the feeling of guilt, for which there was no analgesic he knew of. Unless it was confession.

'How's the head?'

'No better.'

'What you need is another drink. Hair of the dog.'

'I guess so.' He put his arm round Catherine's waist. The

touch of her hip against his as they walked was arousing, adding further to his confusion.

'They're nice people,' he said. They reached the East Gate and entered the gardens. 'Liz and Guy, I mean.'

'Too bloody nice, if you ask me.'

'Are you serious?' They were walking along a broad avenue. Tall trees with smooth grey bark of a species he did not recognize.

'I don't understand people like that. They don't seem to suffer from the usual inadequacies. Guilt. Sexual hang-ups. They remind me of my parents. In fact, they're worse than my parents.'

He was amused at the vituperative accuracy of the description. There *had* been something parental in the solicitude he had been shown at breakfast.

'So tell me about your sexual hang-ups.'

They left the path and began to climb the slopes of the arboretum. Cold sunlight through bare branches threw a net of shadows on the grass. Around them, in the deserted park, wood pigeons were calling, leaves were drifting onto wet lawns. There was a smell of leaf-mould and woodsmoke.

She turned to look at him. 'What is this? Some kind of truth game?' Very lightly she brushed his lips with the tip of her tongue.

'Maybe,' he said unhappily.

'I'll tell you my secrets, if you'll tell me yours,' she said.

'As a matter of fact, I do have something to tell you . . .'

'Oh?'

'I'm married. Does it matter?'

In the flickering autumnal light her face had the secretive quality of a Ghirlandaio portrait. The pale eyes expressionless. The mouth faintly smiling. 'Why should it matter?' she said.

They reached the summit of the hill which stood at the centre of a maze of concentric paths. Below them lay the silent gardens; beyond, the broken skyline of the city. Above the leafless tops of beech trees and slender silver birches rose a thin plume of smoke from a bonfire.

'Catherine – ' The syllables of her name felt unfamiliar on his lips. 'About last night . . .'

She tilted her face to catch the warmth of the weak sunlight, narrowing her eyes against its brightness. 'Lovely view,' she said, 'isn't it?'

A stone archway led into the courtyard of what had once been a formal garden. Stone benches. A trailing vine. A fountain now run dry.

'This place always makes me think of Donne. *Blasted with sighs, surrounded with tears, hither I come to seek the spring* . . .'

'I don't want you to think it wasn't important . . .'

'God, I feel wrecked. I don't suppose you've got a cigarette?'

'No. The fact is . . .'

'Pity.' They were standing in front of the turreted stone building which housed the city's modern art collection. With its weathered, blue-painted shutters, its sundial stained with verdigris, it had the look of a miniature *château*. 'Shall we go inside? There's a Braque or two, a Matisse . . .'

'I wanted to be honest with you.'

'If you don't like Matisse there's some German Expression-ist stuff which might appeal to you.'

'Sure I like Matisse,' he said irritably. He was annoyed at the casualness with which she had heard his confession. It was not that he had expected tears, or even anger, although these would not have been out of place. It was just that her amusement seemed inappropriate, a touch unkind.

In the shuttered hall their eyes took a minute or two to adjust to the gloom, to focus on rectangles of colour, pale blocks of rough-hewn stone, dull cones and cylinders of burnished metal. High above their heads in the domed skylight a fly, waked by the unseasonal sun, crashed its heavy body against the glass. They walked for a while in silence,

34

between rows of images. A Blue Period *Mother and Child*. Arrangements of guitars, bottles and newspapers. An odalisque, beached on her ottoman.

Catherine leaned to examine the surface of a Modigliani portrait – a young woman in a black coat. The eyes in the oval face had been left blank. 'Tell me about your wife,' she said.

He looked at her sharply. 'What do you want to know?'

'I was just wondering why she isn't with you.'

'She's studying to be a teacher.' He was conscious of a certain defensiveness in his tone of voice. As if Virginia's absence were something he had contrived. Which was ridiculous, of course. 'Her course lasts a year.'

'Then I suppose she'll come and join you.' Her tone expressed nothing but detached interest. 'When did you meet her?'

'My freshman year. We were doing the same papers. We used to meet after class and . . . Do you really want to hear this?'

'You must have been very young. Eighteen, or . . .'

'I was nineteen. She's two months younger than me.'

'When did you get married?'

'Right after my finals. We'd been going steady for two and a half years. It was either that or break up, I guess.'

'What's she like?'

'You mean to look at? Pretty, I guess. Dark. About five-two. Her family's Irish originally, and she has these blue eyes and . . .'

'Ah.'

'. . . pale skin. Kind of delicate, you know?' As if conjured up by his words, an image of his wife's face flickered briefly across his consciousness and was extinguished.

'I can imagine.'

He thought he detected an edge of irony in her response.

'Look,' he said, 'I don't want you to think . . . because of

35

what happened last night . . . Christ. What I mean is, this isn't the kind of thing I do very often, you know?'

She smiled at his discomfiture. 'You mean you're not that kind of man after all? What a pity. I was hoping you might be.'

'Seriously . . .'

'You're not the kind of man who has affairs. You love your wife. It was just something that happened.'

'I guess so,' he said lamely.

'Well, that clears that up then.' She slipped her arm through his as they resumed their tour of the gallery.

'Do you still want me to move in?' They had wandered into a room in which a collection of small sculptures was displayed. Maquettes for never-completed works by Gaudier-Brzeska; one of Picasso's constructions of wire and painted plaster; a study for an ornamental fountain by Gabo.

'Why not?' She studied a marble carving of a bird swallowing a fish. It was not clear which of the two was the predator, which the preyed upon. 'You need somewhere to live, don't you?'

'Sure, but . . .'

'It doesn't matter to me if you're married or not. Really. Does that make you feel better about it?'

'Yes . . . that is, I . . .' He swallowed to clear the feeling of constriction in his throat. His voice was hoarser than he'd intended. 'What I'm trying to say is, can we still . . . Oh *God* . . .'

'You can still sleep with me, if you want to,' she said. 'I've no objection.'

In the last room the exhibits were all black, or shades of grey. A *Head of a Girl* by Otto Dix, the pigment so thickly laid on the image became invisible close to. A Jackson Pollock drawing in which the pen-nib seemed in places to have gouged the paper.

'I guess I should have told you before.' Saul paused in front of a charred and twisted Giacometti. 'Like last night . . .'

36

'I can't see what difference it would have made.' She began to walk away from him, her footsteps echoing on the polished floor of the gallery. 'Unless you think I would have enjoyed knowing I was seducing a married man.'

There was no one else in the room, but he glanced quickly over his shoulder.

'I could use some air,' he said, catching up with her. 'It's kind of hot in here.'

They descended the slope towards the glasshouses. Below the summit of the hill, where the sun had not yet reached it, the grass was stiff with frost. As they crossed the wide lawn their footsteps left green tracks. A flock of starlings flew up with a whirring sound.

'I believe in keeping things very unstructured, don't you?' Catherine said, after a silence.

'Oh, sure.' He had the feeling he had been outmanoeuvred. Surely it should have been his prerogative to lay down the ground rules of the affair?

'What I'm saying is, why introduce complications?'

After the frozen stillness of the gardens, the tropical heat inside the glasshouse was overpowering. Above their heads gigantic palms reared towards the light, brushing the ornate wrought-iron and glass roof with ragged fronds. There was a hot, moist smell. The sound of water trickling from an unseen source. Saul half expected to hear the shriek of parrots and small primates in the dense foliage which surrounded them.

'Tell me,' he said, 'have you had many of these . . . unstructured relationships?'

Catherine laughed. 'A few. Does it bother you?'

'Of course not,' he said, piqued that she should suppose him so lacking in sophistication. 'Just curious. Were you ever serious about anyone?'

'What a question.' She made no attempt to answer it, but walked on a few paces ahead of him. Huge fan-like leaves threw ragged shadows on her dress and skin, so that from where he stood she seemed an elusive shape, broken into shifting planes of light and shade.

In the dark red gloom of a basement pub in St Stephen's Street, where shafts of light swept the floor like the blades of a fan as the door swung open to admit a lunchtime clientele of antique dealers, restauranteurs and students, Saul found himself adjusting to infidelity. As a result of his confession – or the beneficial effect of a couple of Bloody Marys – he began to feel a whole lot better about it. Maybe Catherine's attitude was the right one. It didn't matter to her if he was married or not. Whether it mattered to him was something he had yet to work out. If he chose, Saul thought, he could still walk away from the affair. Nobody – except the two people most intimately concerned – need ever know. Yet even as he was considering this possibility, he was making plans to involve himself still deeper.

Catherine's face, a pale mask in the artificial twilight of the red room, seemed to reflect his own mood of calm detachment. He had been disconcerted, certainly, by her initial reaction; now he was beginning to see the advantages of such civilized indifference to convention. Watching her as she lit a cigarette – the match illuminating for an instant a secret face, supposing itself unobserved – he thought how far she was, for him, uncharted territory.

'What are you thinking about?'

'Nothing. No, that's a lie.' She smiled, exhaling a mouthful of smoke. 'I was thinking about sex.'

'Anyone particular in mind?'

'It was a general thought. It occurred to me what a chance you take, giving yourself to another person. I mean, in the nature of things you don't know them until you've . . . *known* them, so to speak. So there's an element of trust . . .'

'Yes . . .'

'. . . or risk, if you like.'

38

'I know. I was thinking the same thing. What do I know about you? Or you about me, for that matter?'

'Nothing. Well, next to nothing. You know the colour of my eyes and my hair. And the way I make love. Oh, I forgot. You can't remember a thing about it.'

'It's starting to come back to me,' said Saul.

'Hi there.' Saul's greeting was answered only by the blind stare of the stone head and an echoing silence, as they entered the London Street apartment. 'They're out, I guess,' he said to Catherine.

'It certainly seems like it.' She was standing in the doorway of the empty room, now his, apparently. He turned so that he was facing her. For a minute neither spoke, transfixed by the moment's potential. He saw, with preternatural clarity, the curve of eyelid, cheek and lip; the pulse beating at her throat. A moment out of time.

'Did I show you my room yet?' he asked. She shook her head, smiling, as he reached for her, sliding his hands down the curve of her ass, pulling her to him. Again, his body hard against hers, his tongue exploring her mouth, he felt a shock of strangeness, an awareness of risk, which heightened his excitement. He pushed her towards the bed.

Virginia would have made him wait: there was always a certain decorum in her undressing. But Catherine, it seemed, was in as much of a hurry as he was, almost ripping a button off his shirt as she undressed him, devouring him with kisses. No less impatient, he pushed her skirt up around her waist. God, he loved women in stockings. That strip of bare flesh between nylon and lace. He drew a line along her inner thigh with his tongue, parallel to that of the taut elastic connecting stocking-top and garter-belt. Reaching the apex, he drummed his tongue on the warm silk, inhaling her sweet-salt smell.

Her dress was an old one – a thrift shop find, he guessed – made of some slippery fabric: crêpe or satin. The zip parted with a whispering sound, then stuck. *Damn*. With a smile in

39

which he detected enjoyment of his predicament, she helped him out. His momentary annoyance was assuaged, however, by the sight of her breasts in black lace; the tactile contrast between smooth white flesh and transparent, slightly scratchy black mesh. The thought of her dressing up with the idea of being undressed was provocative. He slipped the straps down off her shoulders – *nice tits* – circled the hard brown nipple of her right breast with the tip of his tongue, closed his lips around it and tenderly bit it.

'You taste so good,' he murmured, repeating the exercise with the other breast.

As, with hands and tongue, he mapped the contours of her body, his new-found land, calibrating distances from nipples to navel and from navel to vaginal cleft like an artist measuring a drawing. Catherine lay back against the pillow, eyes closed, arms raised above her head. Something about her position – the breasts stretched flat against the ribcage by the lifted arms, the widespread legs, the dark triangle of hair bisected by its glistening slit – made him think of an image once glimpsed in a magazine – not a skin magazine, but a fine-art publication – of a nude woman in high-heeled shoes and black stockings. Gustav Klimt? No . . .

He shucked off his pants and lay down beside her, his erection enormous. Catherine knelt over him, her tongue flicking the head of his penis in a teasing, circular motion, her hair falling over her face, the garter-belt's black harness emphasizing the swooping curves of waist and ass. A study in decadence. She took the shaft in her mouth, swallowing him whole, it seemed. Egon Schiele, he thought.

'That's it . . .'

She raised her head. 'Did you say something?'

'No. Yes. Come here.'

He rolled her onto her back and entered her in a single hard thrust. Becoming, as he did so, part of the composition. An arrangement of limbs, a tangle of discarded clothes; a black and white study of bodies moving in time.

Concentrating on delaying his orgasm, he fixed his thoughts on the images he had looked at earlier that day: an odalisque in Turkish slippers (her lips were parted, her eyes half-closed); a nude in black stockings, spreadeagled on a bed (the way she was moving her hips was driving him insane); a charcoal drawing of lovers, limbs entwined (he felt her legs wrap round him); a kneeling woman, her hair obscuring her face (his heart was pounding, he couldn't hold out much longer); images which resolved themselves, at last, into the woman he held in his arms.

Kissing her, hard, he banged his lip on her teeth and came with the taste of blood in his mouth.

Saul lay on his back on the rumpled bed in the big room flooded with late-afternoon light. Catherine was beside him, curled into the crook of his arm. Her eyes were closed; he wondered if she'd fallen asleep. He could have used some sleep himself.

'I should get going,' he said reluctantly. 'I told Stuart I'd move out by tonight.' He was half hoping, as he spoke, that she might persude him to stay. All she had to do was stretch out her hand. Such an expert hand. He shivered with pleasure, thinking of various ways his departure might be delayed.

But before he could translate his desires into action, Catherine rolled out of his reach, sat up and began to dress. 'I might be out when you get back,' she said.

'Fine.' He knew the disappointment he felt was unreasonable, but was unable to suppress it.

'Only someone's asked me to dinner. And it's a bit late to rearrange it.'

'Oh, sure. Don't even think of it.' He propped himself on one elbow, watching her as she zipped up her dress and brushed her hair, marvelling at the efficiency with which she redefined herself, as if drawing a line beneath what had taken place barely half an hour before, cancelling one incarnation –

41

the naked wanton he had held in his arms – with another, entirely self-possessed being.

'Is it anyone I know?' he could not resist saying.

She looked at him a moment, as if considering not only the question but its implications, then shook her head. 'No,' she said. 'No one you know.'

It was dark by the time he returned to London Street, having packed up his few possessions – clothes, books, toothbrush, razor, a photograph of his wife – and left a note for Stuart. As he unloaded suitcases and cardboard boxes from the trunk of the cab, he looked up at the first floor of the building and saw, with a start, that there was a light on in his room – he was almost sure it was his room. Maybe she'd changed her mind about going out . . .

But when he climbed the stairs, his pulse quickening with anticipation, and pushed open the door of his room, it was to find the Urquharts arranging furniture.

'Oh, there you are.' Liz's face was flushed with the exertion of hanging curtains. 'Well, what do you think?'

'It's very nice.' The bare boards had been covered, he saw, with a worn rug, on which a design of acanthus leaves was dimly visible. A Lloyd Loom chair, its dull green paint flaking in patches, had been placed in one corner, while another was occupied by a battered chest of drawers.

'Guy spotted the chest in the window of the Salvation Army shop,' Liz said, 'and we found the chair on a skip. You wouldn't believe the things people throw away.'

'It looks great. Really.' Saul put down the box he had been carrying, which contained his small collection of reference books and a rough draft of his First Chapter.

'It's an improvement,' Guy said, brushing dust from the palms of his hands with a satisfied air.

Just like my dad closing a deal, Saul thought. What was it Catherine had said? *They're worse than my parents.* 'You shouldn't have gone to so much trouble,' he said.

'Oh, it's no trouble,' Liz smiled. 'Catherine not with you?' she said, after a pause.

'She had to go out. She said she'd be back late.'

'Very late, if I know Catherine,' said Guy with an indulgent glance at his wife.

'A shame she couldn't be here for your first evening.' Liz frowned as she adjusted a lampshade. 'Have you known her long?'

'Not very long.'

'I thought not,' she said vaguely. 'Well, we'll leave you to your own devices for a bit. Dinner's in half an hour.'

'Terrific,' said Saul. 'Say – is it okay if I make a call? Long distance? Only I have to contact someone tonight . . .'

'Ring anyone you like,' Liz said, 'as long as you write it down in the book.'

In his dream Saul went from room to room of an empty building. A palace of some kind. *Be bold, be bold, but not too bold*. The walls of a golden room were covered with pictures, a living tapestry of men and beasts: satyrs, sphinxes, lamiae, women with the faces of birds. As he watched, walls dissolved into leaves and overlapping branches shut out the night. Around him, the foliage was alive with the rustling of feathered creatures, the slithering of scaly monsters. When he turned, the path had vanished. Cold moonlight glittering on half-human shapes, entwined in monstrous love. He felt himself seized. Pinioned.

He opened his eyes. Catherine was sprawled across him. He felt her warm breath on his face, smelt the cigarette smoke in her hair.

'Did I frighten you?' She stripped off her dress in one swift movement, as if sloughing off a skin. 'Listen to your heart,' she said. 'Were you dreaming?'

Her mouth tasted of the wine she had been drinking. She climbed on top of him, taking him into her, moving her hips

43

in lazy circles. Her sharp nails grazed his skin. It seemed to him, still bemused with sleep, as if they had become one body, a thing of scales and claws.

It was midday on Sunday morning before, a little stupefied from lack of sleep, they got out of bed. Liz and Guy were out and the apartment had a pleasantly deserted feel: an echoing box; a theatre of possibilities, Saul thought. He waited for Catherine to finish her bath, dawdling over his second cup of coffee at the big pine table in the kitchen. The uncertainties of the previous evening – the sense of dislocation brought about by unfamiliar surroundings, combined with a faint resentment towards Catherine for abandoning him – were dispelled, to some extent, by a feeling of well-being. The smell of fresh-ground coffee mingled with that of the soap on his skin. A pale wintry light fell through the flawed panes of the window, offering its mild warmth to his upturned face.

From where he sat a prospect of backyards and gardens could be seen – tangles of Michaelmas daisies sprawling under the weight of last night's rain, twisted black limbs of apple trees, broken-down fences, smouldering piles of dead leaves. Fall was his favourite season. He liked its air of shabby elegance, its golds and browns. Its intimations of mortality.

Reflecting on what had happened between him and Catherine, he felt the need to confront her; to put his cards on the table. Certain things had to be established. It was all very well to talk of unstructured relationships, but he was already part of someone else's structure. On the other hand, maybe she was right. Why complicate things more than they were already?

His conversation with his wife the night before had added to his confusion. Had he detected – or only imagined – a note of reproach in her voice when she had first picked up the phone? He had felt his heart beating faster than its normal rate as, feeling that he was saying at once too much and too little, he had described his new accommodation, his interview with Richardson the previous day (how long ago it seemed to

44

him now) and his encounter with Eisenberg. The latter of these episodes he had worked into quite a story, by way of distracting attention, he thought afterwards, from the real story.

'That feels better.' Catherine emerged from the bathroom, naked, her hair wrapped in a towel. A few minutes later she reappeared, wearing her dressing-gown. She poured herself a cup of coffee from the glass jug on the table and sat down opposite him. Sunlight touched her wet hair and the fine bones of her face with muted colour. 'Well,' she said, 'this is very pleasant.'

'I was just thinking the same.' They sat in companionable silence for a few minutes. Saul considered and rejected various approaches to what he wanted to say. What *was* it he wanted to say? 'I have to talk to you,' he said.

'What about?' She gave him an ironic look. 'Don't tell me you've got another wife hidden away somewhere?'

'One's enough, believe me.' He hesitated a moment. 'I called her last night.'

'Did you?' She sipped her coffee slowly, looking at him. 'How is she?'

'She's fine.' He brushed the question away with a small gesture of impatience. 'The fact is, all the time we were talking, I had the feeling I wanted to *tell* her, you know?'

'Tell her what?'

'Oh, come *on*.'

'You had sex with another woman. It happens all the time.'

'Not to me.'

'Look, if it makes you so unhappy we can forget it.'

'If you think that's what I want you must be crazier than I thought. After last night . . .'

'Last night was pretty good.'

'It was more than that. I mean, I've never felt like this before. Almost never. It's so . . . *intense*.'

'You must have felt like that about your wife.'

'I said *almost* never. Anyway, that was different. I'd been

45

going with Virginia for, oh, a couple of months before I realized it was anything special.'

'That's the sign of a mature relationship.'

'Are you saying this isn't?'

'Maybe. Who knows? It's too soon to say.'

'So why not keep things unstructured, huh?' he said drily.

'That's right.' She finished her coffee.

He saw that, far from resolving the question of their relationship, his remarks had only widened the distance between their attitudes to it. It occurred to him that her very remoteness, her refusal to commit herself, were what attracted him.

She caught his eye and smiled. 'What shall we do this afternoon?' she said.

'I can think of one or two things . . .'

'I know. But let's go out.'

'Did you have anywhere in mind?' He was a shade piqued by this rejection.

Catherine rose so that she was standing beside him. She began to wind her fingers in his hair, stroking the long strands back from his forehead and ears, as if trying the effect. 'I always have somewhere in mind. You know, short hair would suit you.'

'My wife likes it long,' he said.

The museum was housed in a magnificent Victorian *palazzo*. Through the vaulted glass ceiling of the main hall the waning light of the November afternoon cast a greenish underwater sheen on everything below: the Chinese fountain with its writhing dragons; the quiet fossils in their glass cases; the dawdling visitors.

Slender cast-iron columns supported two tiers of galleries, which ran the length of the hall and were reached by curving staircases at either end. These structural symmetries were echoed in the building's decorative elements: its arcs and semi-circles repeated in a bas-relief of trilobites, in the flower and leaf motifs around a column, so that the sensation was of having walked into a hall of mirrors.

'Quite a place,' Saul admitted grudgingly.

'It has a good Egyptian section. And a wonderful collection of stuffed birds. Crimson-breasted bee-eaters. Peacock coquettes . . .'

'I've seen enough stuffed birds. Let's look at the mummies.'

Walking amongst *sarcophagi*, Saul found himself translating the day's events into the form of a letter to his wife. *Spent Sunday afternoon in the museum. They have this fantastic bas-relief of Akhenaten. Oh, by the way, I met this girl . . .* The image he had of Virginia seemed distant, diminished by the presence of his lover, whose swaying hips in tight jeans moved ahead of him between the votive cats and funerary objects. He caught up with her, slipped his arm around her waist.

'The underworld seems like a nice place,' he said.

'This is only the afterlife. We haven't reached the underworld yet.'

Passing through a set of heavy glass doors, they found themselves in the geological section of the museum. After the airy spaciousness of the main hall, it seemed a dark cavern; a few seconds elapsed before their eyes adjusted to the gloom. In glass cases around the walls were displayed the fabulous treasures of the earth. Black shapes of ore resembling helmeted heads emerged from the darkness. Volcanic bubbles of haematite, crystals of feldspar, obsidian's ice-flowers. Lazurite risen from the deep cold of mineral sleep.

'Pretty,' Saul said as they paused to examine a rainbow slab of anthracite, its colours shifting with each change of viewpoint. 'Kind of iridescent . . .'

'Iridescent films are more accurately called tarnishes,' Catherine read aloud from a printed card, 'and are due to the presence of impurities . . . That makes sense, I suppose. No beauty without impurity.'

For a while they wandered in a dream of blackness, gazing at purple clusters of amethyst, rose-quartz, chalcedony, jasper, carnelian. Then, tiring of this cold splendour, Saul turned towards his lover. His blind fingers brushed her face, tilting her head back to take his kiss.

In the underworld sleep is ages long, flesh is nothing.

3

There were two things about herself Catherine did not generally admit to. One was that she was in the habit, if you could call it that, of finding playing cards in the street. The other was that she occasionally picked up men for sex.

It was the first and in some ways the more innocuous of the two she found hardest to deal with. She had never, in fact, told anyone about it. It was so stupid, she felt; a symptom of paranoia. The kind of thing that went with extra-terrestrial obsessions and a fixation with tarot cards. Messages from the spirit world. Not her kind of thing at all.

And yet there was no getting away from it. There they were, in the street. Scattered on the pavement like fallen leaves. Jacks, kings, queens, aces, deuces, trays. Hearts, clubs, diamonds, spades. Death-cards and money, dark men and fair, in no sequence that she could discern. Just that in every city and every town in which she found herself there would be, somewhere, a pavement, a street corner, a windy stretch of tarmac on which someone, at some time not too far in advance of her own passing, had dropped a single card, a handful – once a full pack – face up, or showing their blue or green backs.

Next to this intrusion of the uncanny into an otherwise well-ordered life, her episodes with boys seemed a harmless enough distraction.

If she had occasion for self-reproach, it arose from the suspicion that there was something uncontrolled about her predilection for casual sex. Undignified, like a passion for chocolate or cream cakes. It was certainly as hard to resist as any sweet-toothed craving. And there were other reasons to feel guilty.

One of these was the element of exploitation which characterized these brief but intense relationships. Her partners were all of a certain type, a certain social class. Young, poor, working-class, uneducated, inarticulate, sexually unsophisticated. She met them in pubs, in the street, at parties where the booze ran out early and the cheaper sort of drugs were in evidence. She fucked them in cars, against walls, in bus-shelters and in front rooms while their parents slept overhead. She never attempted to see any of them twice, and firmly resisted attempts on their part to see her. Lying where necessary. Inventing jealous husbands, possessive boyfriends, reasons for leaving the country.

She had come to realize (it was this that made her ashamed) that it was not the sex she enjoyed so much as the power, the sense of being in control. It made her wonder what corresponding lack there was in her own make-up, what shameful weakness, that drove her to exercize the power she had – advantages of class, sex, education, money – over those who had none.

She had become aware of this propensity in herself during her first term at Cambridge, at the close of a peculiarly painful affair. She'd made the mistake of confusing desire with emotion; had allowed herself to fall in love. It had been a humiliating episode, the memory of which still made her flinch. When it was over she had assuaged her damaged pride in a series of carnal encounters in which there was little danger of forgetting the distinction between sex and love. Discovering, in the process, a taste for such encounters.

When she met Saul she had been going through a bad patch. Periods of celibacy alternating with those of crazy abandon. Bad sex. Sex with boys in cars. She was sick of sex (she decided then) and sick of herself. She decided a fresh start was in order. And Saul was the *tabula rasa* on which she was going to write.

*

The dichotomy in the novel between form and formlessness, Catherine wrote, *is dramatized as a debate between art and reality: the former conceived as essentially cold, dead, anti-human; the latter as fecund, amorphous –*

'Hey,' said Saul. 'So this is where you're hiding. You don't usually work up here, do you?'

Catherine looked up, suppressing a sigh. In the three weeks since they had started living together, there had hardly been a moment when she and Saul had been apart. They slept together, had breakfast together, walked up to the university together, had lunch together and, as often as not, spent their evenings together. She was beginning to feel that the whole thing was happening a little too fast.

'All the tables downstairs were taken. And it's quiet up here,' she said, putting down her pen with an air of resignation.

'Don't worry, I'm not staying long.' He wandered over to the stacks, took down a volume and blew dust off it. 'What do they keep up here, anyway?'

'Bound theses mostly. Books nobody reads. At least, I've never seen anyone read them.'

'It's certainly quiet. I might come up here to work myself sometime.' He perched himself on the edge of the table, smiling down at her. 'So what are we doing tonight?' he said.

'I said I'd go to that poetry reading of Robin's. I assumed you weren't coming.' She threw him a mischievous look. 'Of course, if you want to come, I'm sure Robin won't mind . . .'

'Do me a favour. The more I hear about that guy's poems the less I want to hear.' He shrugged. 'I have some work to finish anyway. How about if I meet you later? We could pick up something to eat.'

'Gillian said there'd be food at their place.'

'What time does it start?'

'Eight-ish. But I really don't think – '

'Terrific. We'll have time for a drink before you go.' He

leaned across the desk, nuzzled her ear. 'It's the least you can do, since you're abandoning me for a bunch of poets.'

'Alright. One drink.' The mild exasperation she had been feeling evaporated in amusement. At least he knew what he wanted, she thought. And whatever her misgivings about the affair, she had to admit that certain aspects of it couldn't have been better. The sex, for one.

'Admit it. You can't resist me.' He brushed his mouth across hers. 'I'll pick you up at six.'

'Six-thirty.'

'Oh, this *woman*.' He appealed to an invisible jury. 'She's trying to drive me wild . . . Six-thirty. And don't be late.'

Catherine read through the sentence she had just written, then crossed it out. For the next few minutes she made an effort to focus her attention on the book whose themes and situations she was attempting to analyze, but found herself distracted by thoughts of her own situation. It seemed to her that Saul was expecting too much of the relationship, encroaching too far upon her autonomy. Asking questions. Wanting to know things about her she wasn't sure she wanted him to know. Had she ever been in love? What was the guy's name? Had there been others? How many? Hadn't she ever wanted to settle down?

Her response to most of these questions had been evasive, not because she was ashamed of the truth, but because she suspected that frankness would entail justifying her actions. And that was something for which she felt little inclination. Outside the plate-glass windows of the library the bare branches of trees in George Square lost their definition in the gathering dusk. The sky deepened to blue, faded to black.

On Sunday nights Saul wrote to his wife. In these letters, which she never read, Catherine knew he was in the habit of describing the events of their life together. The daily walk up to the university, the breaks for coffee, lunch and tea in the English faculty canteen, the meetings with supervisors, the evenings with friends and the Sunday excursions to museums and art galleries were recorded with meticulous thoroughness. Occasionally he consulted her on a point of detail.

'What was the name of that painter again? The portrait of a young man. You said it looked a bit like me.'

'Andrea del Sarto.'

Sometimes he asked her to spell certain words. *Porphyry*. *Triptych*.

'And what was that place we went to? That little room in the tower . . .'

'The Camera Obscura.'

They had climbed the spiral stair to stand like initiates at some arcane rite around the concave white table across which phantasmal shapes – lovers kissing in the street, the shiny carapaces of cars, a child running – moved in silence, growing sharper or indistinct according to the changing light. Observing, through this magic mirror, the comings and goings of other people, each oblivious of observation, gave them a sense of power that seemed almost immoral. As if by reaching out a finger one could rearrange the pieces – houses, trees, cars, people – at will. Or, growing tired of the game, knock them off the board altogether.

'I have to put something in my letters, don't I?' he'd said, a touch defensively, when she'd teased him about it. 'She tells me about the things she does, the people she sees . . .'

'Ah, but does she tell you everything?'

'How would I know? And anyway, I don't tell her *everything* . . .'

'I should hope not.'

To anyone reading the letters it must have seemed like the complete picture. And so it was, thought Catherine. Complete except for one thing. It amused her to think of herself being, as it were, painted out of the composition. She was the shadowy figure in the background whose presence had been obscured by drapery or a detail of landscape, whose features

53

had been altered from those of a dressed corpse to those of a smiling bride. Only with the removal of the surface layer, the false image, would the true picture be revealed.

The telephone conversations Saul had with his wife on Sunday nights offered a different kind of entertainment. It was like hearing one part of a piece of music scored for two instruments. Half an aria. There was a desire, on the part of the listener, to supply the missing part. Catherine, lying in bed with the radio turned down low, would piece together, from the fragments of whispered argument she could hear through the open door, what was being said by the invisible woman on the other end of the line.

'What do you mean? Of *course* I love you . . .'

Afterwards, in the dull hinterland of Sunday evening, Saul was abstracted, depressed. He would let slip information about Virginia – her moods, her circumstances – which Catherine hoarded as if these could provide her with the clue to some as yet undefined puzzle. In this way she learned certain things about the other woman: the date of her birth (a few days after Catherine's own), her dress size, her taste in clothes. She knew when Virginia was depressed, or suffering from period pains, or having trouble writing an essay. She could envisage (from Saul's description) the apartment he had shared with Virginia during the first year of their marriage and where she was still living, sub-letting to another teacher, while she pursued her studies.

It was possible, also, to deduce a good deal about her rival's sexual preferences from the way the partner they had in common behaved in bed, but this was a discovery Catherine kept to herself. Her interest in Virginia was, in any case, a source of irritation to Saul. It was as if he felt it was inappropriate, somehow. Jealousy would have been forgive-able; curiosity was not. Yet Catherine found it hard to restrain herself from asking about Virginia. The more she knew, the more she wanted to know. Piece fitted onto piece in the jigsaw that was Virginia's life. Each day a little more emerged: the curve of a cheek, the outline of a shoulder-blade, the pattern of a dress. A detail which might have been a patch of sky or the sea.

'So these other guys . . . How many were there?'

'I've no idea.'

'What do you mean, you've no idea? You slept with them didn't you?'

'I didn't sleep with them, I fucked them. And I wasn't counting.'

'You're incredible, you know?'

'Anyway, I don't see that it matters how many there were. I haven't fucked – or slept with – anyone else since I met you.'

'I just don't understand how you could do that to yourself.'

'You don't understand much, do you?'

'I mean, can't you see how self-destructive that kind of behaviour is?'

'Spare me the psychoanalysis. I'd never have told you if I'd thought you were going to get so upset.'

'I'm not upset . . .'

'Let me ask you something. Haven't you ever slept around?'

'Well, sure, but . . .'

'But what?'

'That was different.'

'Why? Because you're a man and I'm a woman, I suppose.'

'I didn't say that.'

'You didn't have to.'

They were in a club in St Stephen's Street which Catherine liked for its seedy ambiance and because its medley of disco standards included an occasional dance track from the early sixties. The decor was reminiscent of a tropical island paradise, incorporating Easter Island statuettes of polystyrene and a false ceiling of fishing nets supporting a catch of plastic barracudas and swordfish.

'My God, what a tacky place,' Saul had said when they arrived.

They'd pushed their way through the crowd towards the bar, which was thatched with palm fronds and garlanded with cockle shells, ordered drinks from a sullen waitress in a grass skirt and sat at a table shaped like an upturned rum cask, overlooking the dance floor on which girls in backless dresses and boys in skintight T-shirts and baggy jeans stamped and shimmied to the rhythms of some antediluvian disco queen. It was in these convivial surroundings that they'd begun their quarrel. Not at first recognizing it as such.

'Isn't it wonderful? A kind of time-capsule of the early seventies.' Catherine chased a sliver of lime around the rim of her glass with a cocktail stick. 'It reminds me of my misspent youth.'

'So tell me about it,' Saul said. 'This misspent youth of yours.'

She wasn't sure afterwards if it had been the effect of the alcohol or just that she was tired of evading his questions which made her decide to take him at his word. So she had told him as much as she could remember of her disreputable past. At least he would no longer be able to say he didn't know everything there was to know about her. And now he was avoiding her gaze, his expression betraying hurt and anger, dejectedly stirring the ice-cubes at the bottom of his glass with a miniature plastic sword.

The mechanistic throbbing of mass-market dance music gave way to the stripped down rhythms of R & B. 'Hey,' said Catherine, 'I like this one. Let's dance.'

'I don't feel like dancing.'

'Of course you do.' She drew him out onto the floor, sliding her arms around his neck, humming the lyrics of the song, a jaded ballad, as she moved her hips in time to the music.

Catherine ran into Gillian Orr outside the faculty library.

'How's work?'

'Okay. How about you?'

Gillian frowned. 'Don't ask. This place is impossible. I

56

mean, after Cambridge . . .' Her fingers sketched a dying fall. Catherine adjusted her expression into something resembling sympathetic agreement. Her friend's snobbish contempt for anything that wasn't Cambridge bored and irritated her.

'If it wasn't for Rob I think I'd find it all too depressing for words.'

'How is Robin?'

'Busy. You know Robin. He had a letter from Flynn the other day, saying how much he enjoyed *Open Wounds*.'

'Really?' said Catherine. 'That's nice.' W. H. Flynn was the Cambridge don and avant-garde poet who had supervised Robin's dissertation on Eliot.

'He wants Rob to submit a poem or two for inclusion in an anthology of new writing he's editing for Faber. Only of course Rob says nothing he's done lately is any good. So he's been sitting up till two in the morning every night for the past week trying to come up with something for the bloody book.'

'Poor Robin. Look, I really ought to be getting back . . .'

'You've got time for a coffee. There's something I wanted to ask you.'

Catherine hesitated. She had a feeling she knew what was coming. They began to descend the stairs towards the canteen. A pervasive reek of burnt milk and stale ashtrays greeted them as they pushed open its swing doors. They paid for their coffee and sat down.

'So tell me,' said Gillian, narrowing her eyes as she took the first drag on a cigarette, 'how long have you been seeing Saul Meyer?'

'That depends on what you mean by seeing.'

'You know what I mean. Are you living with him?'

'To an extent,' said Catherine.

'Well, if you're going to be evasive . . .'

'He moved into London Street a month ago. We have sex. But we're not really living together, if you see the distinction.'

'I must say I think it's rather an academic one.' Gillian

stirred her coffee, banging the spoon on the rim of the cup as if her irritation could be alleviated by this small act of violence. 'I mean, you're either living with him or you're not. You do know he's married?'

'I believe he may have mentioned it.'

'I just thought you ought to know. Not that it's any of my business, of course . . .'

'Hey – ' Saul came in, saw them and waved. 'I had an idea I'd find you here,' he said to Catherine. 'Measuring out your life in coffee spoons, as usual. Hi Gillian. How's it going?'

'Things could be worse I suppose.'

'Exactly my philosophy. Thank God there's only a week to go.'

'I imagine you'll be going home for Christmas, won't you?' said Gillian with a small tight smile. Saul looked at Catherine. This was something they had not yet discussed.

'I guess so,' he said. 'That is I . . .'

'Of course you're going home,' said Catherine. There was a silence.

Gillian pushed back her chair. 'I must go.' She began to walk away, thought better of it and returned to the table. 'Rob and I were thinking of having some people round next Friday, before everyone leaves. A sort of pre-Christmas celebration. You'll come, won't you? Both of you.'

'I can't answer for Saul,' said Catherine, 'but I should be able to make it. I'm not going down till the weekend.'

'I'll be there,' said Saul.

'Super.' Gillian's smile betrayed a certain malicious enjoyment of the situation. 'About eight then.'

'What *is* it about that couple?' Saul said, when Gillian was barely out of earshot. 'Somehow I get the feeling they've got it in for me.'

'Just your paranoia,' said Catherine.

An afternoon in December. Melting snow fell from rooftops, froze in the act of falling. Curtains stirred in the breeze from the open window where a naked man stood, smoking a cigarette. It was a recently acquired habit, which did not yet suit him, Catherine thought. He had an affected way of holding the thing, like a character in a French film.

'Saul?'

'Mm hm?'

'When are you leaving?'

They were in his room, which retained, despite certain alterations and additions (a mirror, a bookcase, a picture or two) the air of a temporary encampment, an impression enhanced by its state of disarray. Clothes were strewn on the chair and across the end of the bed; piles of library books awaiting return covered the table; an open suitcase lay on the floor.

'I don't know for sure.' Saul yawned and stretched, a contented animal. 'I guess Saturday. It depends if I can get a flight.'

'Fine.' Catherine watched her lover through half-closed eyes. From where she lay, too idle to move, she could see the long curve of his spine, the lazy movement as he flexed his shoulders. The bunched, muscular shape of his upper torso was outlined against the blank rectangle of the window like a charcoal drawing on white paper. At the base of his spine a feathery wedge of dark hair disappeared between the cheeks of his buttocks, a careless smudge from the artist's thumb.

'I don't have to go.' His tone was deliberately casual. He was testing her, she felt, trying to force an admission. *I want you to stay . . .*

'Of course you do.'

'I could just stay here. With you.'

She thought for a minute of calling his bluff. *Alright. Stay then.* But thought better of it. 'What about your wife?'

He shrugged. 'She's got to know sooner or later.' Flakes of ash dropped from his smouldering cigarette onto the sill and blew back into the room.

'I can't imagine why.' He was making it harder for both of

59

them, Catherine felt. Trying to involve her in his guilt. 'I should have thought the arrangement worked rather well,' she said, keeping her voice light. 'She's in New York. I'm here. Neither of us makes unreasonable demands. It doesn't seem to me you have any grounds for complaint.'

He stared at her, as if trying to work out whether or not she was serious. Deciding, in the end, that she was not. 'You know something? You're totally amoral.'

That was better, thought Catherine. At least he'd dropped the note of existential gloom. 'I wouldn't have said totally.'

In the street a car door slammed. Heels clicked on the pavement. The red-haired hippy chick, a throwback to the Summer of Love, emerged from the basement across the street. Today she was wearing a scarlet embroidered dress sewn all over with tiny mirrors, which glittered in the sun. He watched her walk to the corner – *nice ass* – then turned from the window. The breeze made the small hairs on his body stand on end, as if a cold finger had grazed his spine.

'The fact is,' he said resentfully, 'I feel like such a jerk. Lying to her.'

'Come back to bed.'

As they began to make love she had the feeling his mind was elsewhere. There was something mechanical about his caresses, as if he had disengaged himself from what his body was doing. It was something she'd done often enough herself. She ran her hands down his back, feeling the smooth elastic tension of his skin. The kick as he entered her. It was a good sensation, she thought. Being filled. Fulfilled. Although on this occasion it did nothing to assuage the emptiness she was feeling. Afterwards he rolled over and lay on his back, sighing with post-coital *tristesse*. A slanting, late-afternoon light filled the room. All the scene lacked, she reflected, was the subtitles.

'It sounds stupid,' he said, his gaze fixed on the ceiling, 'but we've always been honest with each other, Virginia and me.'

'I don't call that being honest.'

When he said nothing she turned on her side so that she was looking down into his face. A sullen mask. The eyes, twin mirrors, giving back her own reflection.

'Don't you think you should at least tell her to her face? If you must tell her.'

Saul frowned. A couple of minutes ago he had shocked himself by offering to leave his wife for her and now she was making him feel like a criminal. *Jesus*.

'You obviously think it's a bad idea,' he said sulkily, 'so let's just forget it, okay?'

'What I think or don't think isn't important.'

There were times, he thought, when her tone of moral detachment drove him crazy. Why couldn't she admit she had feelings like everyone else?

'Tell her. Only don't pretend you're being honest. You don't know what the word means.'

He stretched his arms above his head and there was a flash of wings as the tattooed eagle on his forearm flexed its pinions. He'd had it done for a bet, in high school, he'd told Catherine. His parents had been furious, but by then it was too late. Of course he regretted it, now. It was the kind of thing you almost always regret, once the initial impulse is past. But what can you do? You're stuck with it – hearts and arrows, skull and crossbones, whatever. You can't undo the art of ink and needles.

'Since when did you get to be such a moralist?' he said.

4

Christmas, season of *ennui* and suicide attempts, passed without incident for Catherine. It was the same this year as always: three weeks of wearing plaid skirts, going for long walks and ignoring her mother's pointed remarks about marriage. She'd tried not to think too much about Saul. The last few days they'd spent together had passed in a blur of packing and travel arrangements. The Orr's party had only exacerbated the vague depression both had been feeling. On the last day they had exchanged phone numbers, knowing it was unlikely either would get in touch; although for a couple of days after her return home, Catherine had experienced a stab of emotion – it felt like fear – each time the telephone rang.

Returning from Kent a few days into the New Year, she was disconcerted, nonetheless, by the sharp feeling of disappointment which assailed her as she opened the door of his room to find he had not yet returned. Evidently he was in no hurry to surrender the comforts of married life. The Urquharts were still away in the Highlands. She tried a couple of friends' numbers before giving up the search for companionship. There was always work, if she needed distraction from thoughts of her absent lover. She spent most of the next two days in the library, or curled up in front of the fire in the living room at London Street. Consoling herself with fiction.

On the morning of the third day the telephone rang; an invitation to a party, from someone she'd given her number to a couple of months back. She accepted, thinking that being with other people might lift her spirits, although in this she was mistaken as it turned out. She'd ended up drinking too much and sleeping on a stranger's floor.

Not an auspicious start to the year, she thought, breakfasting on black coffee in a café in the Grassmarket. Although it was not yet eight, the place was crowded. Men in donkey jackets were eating large fried breakfasts before starting work, or after finishing work. A group of women in overalls were drinking tea, after cleaning the National Library from top to bottom. At a table across the aisle from her own a young woman with a thin, colourless face fed pieces of doughnut dipped in tea to a small child. In the warm haze of cigarette smoke and steam from the espresso machine, Catherine let her thoughts drift.

She had no intention of getting involved again. At least, not to the extent where extricating herself might prove difficult. It had been clear from the start that there could be no long-term commitment between her and Saul. And, after all, wasn't it what she wanted – an informal arrangement? No demands, no promises, she decided, extinguishing her cigarette.

She'd been in the Reading Room an hour or so when Saul came in, saw her and came over. He looked different, she thought, or perhaps in the intervening three weeks since they'd last met she'd forgotten his face. It seemed to her there was a guardedness in his approach, as if he were monitoring his response, checking this present incarnation against some earlier image he had of her. As she was doing with him, of course. They conversed in whispers.

'Hi.'

'When did you arrive?'

'Last night.'

Last night. Shit. That stupid party.

'You were out.'

'Yes.'

'Did you want a coffee?'

She nodded. Her eyes hurt from too long under the flickering strip-lights. When she closed them sentences and paragraphs printed themselves on her retina. She wished now she'd bothered to go home and change. She felt like something that had crawled out from under a stone.

'Let's go.'

A fine cold rain that was turning to snow powdered their clothes and hair as they descended the steep spiral of Victoria Street.

'God I hate this climate.' Saul hunched his shoulders inside his lightweight raincoat as they climbed the creaking stairs to the dark, soot-smelling parlour of the Robert Burns Coffee Shoppe. 'I mean, how do these people stand it?'

'You get used to it, I suppose. Or you die.'

'I think death might be the easy option. When did you get back?'

'A few days ago.'

'I didn't hear you come in last night.'

'I went to a party.'

'Have fun?'

'Not really.'

An elderly waitress brought coffee in thick white cups. Catherine, tasting it, found it was lukewarm. They were the only occupants of the place, which was furnished with an assortment of broken-backed chairs and rickety tables. Above the soot-blackened fireplace hung a portrait of Robert Burns, evidently painted after a rough night. The poet's long hair was dishevelled, his lips twisted in a dissolute sneer. In his hand he held a quill pen, as if caught in the act of dashing off a couple of stanzas. *O whistle and I'll come to you.*

'How was New York?'

'Cold. Only nothing like this. Blue skies. Sunshine. Remember sunshine?'

'If I try very hard.'

'God, I wish you could've been there.' He took her hand across the table, his eyes bright with sudden emotion. 'I missed you a lot. A couple of times I almost called you, just to hear the sound of your voice. I kept thinking about you. Wondering what you were doing.'

'Eating too much mostly. Going to church . . .'

'You go to *church*?'

'It's one of the main attractions of going home. All that High Anglican ritual. How's Virginia?'

'She's okay. Oh, *damn* – ' A rash movement, as he leaned towards her, upset the precarious equilibrium of the table and with it his coffee. 'This is too bad.' He dabbed ineffectually at his stained trousers. 'Now I'll have to sit there all afternoon with Richardson staring at my wet crotch.'

'It'll dry. What time are you seeing him?'

'Three o'clock. We can have lunch first. God, it's so good to be back . . .'

'So did you tell her?'

'Tell who?' He was playing for time. 'You mean Virginia?' Her gaze was disconcerting. 'No. The fact is . . . I didn't get an opportunity.'

'You mean you lost your nerve.' A momentary disappointment gave way to relief. Things could go on as they were.

'I told you, there was no time.' He sounded aggrieved. 'I mean, we hardly spent any time together the whole vacation. You know how it is, when you haven't seen your friends in a while. A whole bunch of guys dropped in . . .'

'Sounds like fun.'

'We had to go see her parents and my parents and — what do you mean, *fun*? It was terrible. All the time I have this . . . this *guilt* hanging over me and I have to act like everything's okay . . . You call that *fun*?'

'Did you sleep with her?' Her interest, she told herself, was purely academic. Of course she didn't care one way or the other. But she had to know.

'She's my wife, isn't she? Of course I slept with her. What did you expect me to do? Ask for separate rooms?'

'I mean did you have sex?'

'Catherine, I hadn't seen her for two and a half months . . .'

'I know. It was an unfair question.' *What was it like, the*

66

first time? Did you compare her with me? 'Don't look like that. I think you did the right thing. Not telling her, I mean.'

'It's just that all the time I was with her I felt like such a bastard, you know?'

'It's the price you pay for illicit sexual gratification.' *No demands, no promises.*

'I guess so.' He smiled at her, showing his beautiful teeth. With his dark eyes, his big nose, his too-long hair, his face had the look of one glimpsed in an old newsreel. Haunted, birdlike, disappearing into shadow.

'You know what? You haven't kissed me yet,' he said.

Killing time in the university bookshop, Saul had a momentary attack of vertigo. In his pocket was the letter he had received that morning from his wife – *Darling, just to say how much I enjoyed our time together* – in his hand, the copy of *Eros and Civilization* he was about to buy for his lover. He must be crazy, he thought, to have let things go this far. More than ever he regretted his cowardice in saying nothing to Virginia of his affair. When he had got off the plane at JFK he'd had every intention of telling her. But his first sight of her face – so sweet and trusting – as she waited for him at the Arrivals gate had fatally undermined his resolution. And now he was stuck with the consequences . . . *It was wonderful to hear all about your life in Edinburgh. I only wish I could share it with you* . . .

'Well *hi*,' said a voice he knew. 'How's life treating you these days?' Robert's arms were full of books and he held a typed reading list in his free hand.

'Okay I guess. How about you?'

'Oh, great, just great,' said Robert. 'As a matter of fact, Professor Richardson's asked me to help out on some footnotes for the edition of *Astrophel and Stella* he's doing for the OUP.'

'That's good.'

'I have to admit I was pretty knocked out when he asked

me.' Robert's eye fell on the Marcuse. 'What's that you've got there? Doesn't look like Spenser studies to me . . .'

'It's for a friend.'

'For a minute there you had me worried,' Robert said, with heavy playfulness. 'So how was your vacation?'

'It was fine.' Saul edged towards the counter, the book in his hand. 'Say, Robert, I really have to run. I'm meeting somebody.'

'Wife okay?'

'She's fine. How's . . .'

'Carol. Carol's fine too. Say, you really should drop in one evening. I guess you must get pretty lonely. I don't know how you stand it . . .'

'Oh, I try to keep busy,' said Saul, uncomfortably aware of what Robert, with his uxorious ways, his serious disposition, would say if he knew the truth.

In George Square Saul saw Catherine coming towards him through a crowd of people and felt a shock of pleasure, mingled with a desire to assert his possession of her. He wanted to take her in his arms in front of all these people: students pouring out of lecture rooms, elderly dons on bicycles. Let them all see, and envy him.

'Busy day?'

She nodded, falling into step beside him. He saw, with a rush of tenderness, the dark circles under her eyes, her pale mouth.

'You look tired. Want to stop for a drink somewhere?'

'If you like.'

She took his arm. Turning into North Bridge Street they were caught by a gust of wind which blew them along together like starlings caught in a cross-current. The rain had turned to snow. Cold flakes clung to their eyelashes with a touch like feathers. Breathless, blinded by tiny splinters of ice, they surrendered themselves to the slipstream.

*

In the morning they woke to the bleached light of snowfall. The street and all its familiar angularities had been obliterated. Cars lay buried under a thick white crust, each blurred shape an indicator of where the street had been. It was quiet – the intense silence of a desert citadel buried by sandstorms or a city after nuclear attack.

'It looks like we're snowbound. They'll need a helicopter to rescue us.' Catherine turned from the window. The milky light cast bluish shadows on her face and neck and on the curve of her breast where her robe fell open. Saul watched her from the bed as she moved about the room, picking up scattered clothes from the night before. He reached for her as she passed, pulling her down on top of him.

'Who wants to be rescued?' He hadn't known till he'd said it how much he enjoyed being lost, stranded without a map in a foreign land. Making love was like that, he thought idly: a form of self-abnegation. Losing oneself in another. Slowly, with a cartographer's patience, he began to caress her. *La petite mort.* He felt himself run to meet it.

It was late afternoon before they decided to get up. In the big living room Liz sat in front of the fire, finishing off some marking. She looked up, smiling. 'I didn't hear you come in.'

'We didn't go out. The snow was our excuse.'

'Isn't it lovely? When it's like this I wish we had a cottage in the hills somewhere, just Guy and me, and a good supply of malt whisky. No need to see anybody, no need to do anything. Close the shutters and wait till spring.' She pushed away the stack of exercise books and stood up. 'Anyone fancy some toast?'

'Sounds good.'

Saul stood at the window, watching the white flakes converge in endlessly spiralling formations. A mirror shattering in slow motion. The effect was hypnotic. For a minute or two he forgot himself, lost in that whirling immensity. Since his return from New York, a sense of unreality had pervaded his waking thoughts, so that there were times, like now, when he had to remind himself he wasn't dreaming.

It was as if he were living not one life but two, each as rich in complexity and incident as the other. Only a few days ago he had been with Virginia, sleeping in her bed, eating at her table, discussing the future with her as calmly as if he had nothing else on his mind. Now he was here with Catherine; an existence less structured perhaps, but no less intense. She was real. The falling snow, the warmth of the room behind him, the smell of burning toast wafting through from the kitchen – these, too, were real enough. The only unreal thing was himself. As if his identity, stretched too thin by the exigencies of playing a double role, had been left ghost-like, a shadow.

'What's the matter?' Catherine touched his arm.

'Nothing.' He forced a smile. 'Just tired, I guess. Delayed jet-lag.'

'Or guilt. You think about things too much. Don't think.'

'I wish it was that easy.' But he knew she was right. Living in a parallel universe meant you had to think parallel thoughts. Not mix them up. Guilt was the point at which one set of conditions bled into the other, corrupting both. He resolved to have no more to do with guilt.

The midwinter sun turned the snow-covered fields to sheets of fire; the sky was incandescent, so blue it hurt to look at it.

In the snow, someone had written *SMOKE*. An invocation, Catherine thought. Snow had soaked through the soles of her thin boots; her hands in their wet woollen gloves burned with cold.

'Some say the world will end in ice,' she murmured in Saul's ear as, following the blue indentations of others' footsteps, they crossed the wide white surface, slipping and sliding and holding on to one another.

'Fire,' said Saul, 'not ice. Ice comes after.'

'I'll take your word for it.'

Behind them lay the city, an image etched on glass; beyond, the blue line of hills. As they walked their breath formed flamboyant clouds in front of them, each icy lungful turned to steam in the body's alembic. Air to water. Ice to fire. In the middle of the dazzling plain they stopped; embraced. Warm-blooded figures in a frozen landscape.

'Sometimes I feel my life is totally out of control, you know?' said Saul.

Sitting opposite him in the faculty canteen, Magda looked unimpressed. 'You should have my problems. Did I tell you that crazy Muriel's latest idea? She wants a reconciliation. Like they've only been separated two years and they hate the sight of each other but she thinks it could work, you know?'

'What does Donald think?'

'Oh God, who knows? I don't think even Donald knows.' Resting her elbows on the table, Magda gathered handfuls of black and white hair, drawing it back from her forehead. 'So aren't you two getting on, or what?' she said, swallowing a yawn.

'We get on fine. She just refuses to discuss the situation.'

'What *is* the situation? Are you going to divorce Virginia?'

There were times, Saul thought, when his friend's candour verged on brutality. 'I don't know. That's what I want to discuss.'

'Does Virginia want a divorce?'

'No. I mean, she doesn't know anything about it.'

Magda opened her eyes very wide. 'Oh, baby. You *are* in a mess, aren't you?' She looked at her watch. 'Hey, got to run. I'm giving a seminar on *The Dead* in fifteen minutes.'

The fact was, Saul thought gloomily as he finished his sandwich, a confection of spongy white bread and synthetic-tasting cheese that turned to mush in the mouth, none of his friends understood what he was going through. In the month since his return his moods had fluctuated between euphoria and despair. Just as he thought he had reached equilibrium, something – a stray thought, a treacherous memory – would trip him from behind.

There were days when radical solutions seemed the only ones worth considering. He would ask Virginia for a divorce. He would commit himself wholly to his new life. He and Catherine would find a place together, where they would pursue their studies. They might, given time, even return to the States together. He didn't feel he was cut out for a life of exile.

In envisaging this scenario, however, he was troubled by certain inconsistencies. What if Virginia refused to accept the role assigned to her? She could make things very difficult. He imagined tears, recriminations. Rehearsed arguments with her in his head. He was young. They were both young. They had made a false start. All that was necessary was that they should unmake it and start over. That was what life was all about.

Catherine presented another set of problems. For it was clear from things she had said – or not said – that her version of what the future held was radically different from his own. Sometimes he got the feeling that he himself didn't feature at all in her projections. The very things which bothered Saul about their relationship – its unstructuredness, its open-endedness – were the things with which she seemed most at home. She seemed not to understand the passion for order, for symmetry, which lay behind his anatomizing of the affair, as if by imposing a structure – divorce, marriage – he could establish a measure of consistency on the random patterns of their lives.

Towards the end of February the thaw set in. The weather grew milder and the city assumed another aspect. Grey stone, washed with sunlight, lost its funereal look. Bare branches suddenly acquired a covering of palest green. For the first time since his arrival, Saul was prepared to admit the place had something to be said for it. It was like discovering that the woman who had occupied the seat opposite his in the library all winter, swathed in scarves and with a permanent head cold, was a beauty.

He finished his chapter on the *Book of Chastity* the day before his twenty-fifth birthday and was taking Catherine out to celebrate. Dinner at the Oyster Bar, followed by a late showing of the new Buñuel. He had arranged to meet her in the bar and, inevitably, she was late. As he finished his drink and signalled to the barman to bring another, he reflected that her behaviour was absolutely typical. It expressed, he felt, a contempt for order. Another, related, fault was her sloppiness about personal hygiene. Used tampons, swollen with blood, left on the edge of the basin, lipstick smears on the pillow. It drove him crazy.

'I'm late.'

'That's right.' But he forgot his annoyance in the pleasure of seeing her again. She was wearing a tight black skirt and the red blouse he liked. 'Do you want a drink here, or shall we order one at the table?'

'Let's have one here. There's lots of time, surely?'

'If you say so.'

'Don't be cross. Here. I've got something for you.'

It was a flat square package. A record, of course. His first thought when he unwrapped it was one of mild disappointment. Robert Johnson. A Mahler symphony would have been more to his taste. But then he saw her face.

'Recorded in San Antonio, November 1936,' she said, 'in a hotel room.'

'Where else?'

'Do you like it?'

From the record sleeve the gaunt face of a young black man in a high collar and dark suit stared back at him. 'Little Queen of Spades', he read. 'Me and the Devil Blues'. 'Love in Vain'. 'I love it,' he said untruthfully.

73

'Almost forgot . . .' Her kiss left a blurred smudge of red at the corner of his mouth. 'Happy birthday.'

'I can't think of a way I'd rather spend it.' It occurred to him as he spoke that Virginia might try to call him tonight. He pushed the thought from his mind. 'Are you ready to order? The film starts in forty-five minutes. If we hurry we can just make it.'

'What are we seeing again? Something about an obscure object . . .'

'Of desire. You'll love it. Finish your drink.'

'You'll be going home at Easter, won't you?' Catherine said as they walked home that night down Hanover Street. The lights of New Town scattered below them, a broken necklace.

'I haven't made up my mind.'

'Wouldn't Virginia think it was strange if you didn't go? Or is she planning to come over here?'

The windows of houses they passed as they descended the wide, sloping street framed partial views of other lives: a woman turning in a doorway; people playing cards around a green baize table; someone pulling a curtain across.

'She's too busy right now. They have exams next month. Why do you want to know, anyway?'

Some of the rooms were empty: beautiful sets for events about to happen; or never to happen. Fires burned in marble fireplaces, flowers bloomed in tall vases, lamps had been lit against some eventual return. In one room a game of chess was in progress, in another a book lay open on the arm of a chair; mute objects waiting until players or reader were ready to resume.

'I thought if you decided to stay we could go away for a few days. Liz said we could use their place in Argyll . . .' When he did not reply at once she turned to look at him. 'Don't you think it's a good idea?'

As they turned into Great King Street the night wind

caught them, blowing their words away, so that each had to shout to be heard.

'I think it's a terrific idea. I just can't believe you're suggesting it. I mean, are you sure you know what you're saying? You want to spend some time with me? Alone? Away from your friends? Nothing but mountains and trees for company?'

'Don't push your luck,' said Catherine, laughing, her hair blown across her face, 'or I might just change my mind.'

Over the next few weeks, Saul got better acquainted with Robert Johnson. The dour young face above the stiff collar became a familiar one, regarding him with an expression alternately impassive and accusing, from the faded 1920s photograph on the record sleeve.

> I got a kind-hearted woman
> Do anything in this world for me . . .

The voice with its rising and falling cadences, its broken rhythms, entwined itself with the moment: the sunlight falling through half-open shutters into the big room, Catherine's presence beside him, the sensation of her hair brushing his face as she leaned against him, the touch of her smooth bare arm.

> Got a kind-hearted woman
> Do anything in this world for me,
> But these evil-hearted women
> Man, they will not let me be . . .

All these things – the plangent sound of guitar and voice, the touch of a bare arm, the broad swathe of sunlight across a floor sparkling with dust motes – would come back to him with shocking clarity on the occasion when, years later, he heard the song again.

She's a kind-hearted woman,
She studies evil all the time.
She's a kind-hearted woman,
She studies evil all the time.
You'll have to kill me, baby,
Just to have it on your mind.

5

At 30,000 feet the city was an exploded star, its points radiating from the volcanic detritus at its centre to the border regions, the mountains, the sea. The plane circled in to land, descending into a vortex of connecting lines and broken radii. These resolved themselves, at a lower altitude, into streets, squares, circuses. The illusion now was of a relief map: hills, lakes, churches, houses and municipal parks illuminated in perfect detail by the rays of the setting sun.

Another few minutes and they would be landing. Sitting in the window seat of the 747, Virginia considered the letter. Her fine-drawn brows tightened as she regarded the translucent onion-skin pages, the meticulous, sloping characters with which they were covered, whose meaning grew more, not less, opaque with every reading.

My dear Virginia . . . It was unlike Saul to be so formal in his letters to her. Usually he addressed her as Baby, Sweetheart or Darling Gina, a diminutive which suggested, he said, the Italianate quality of her looks, her expression of stony innocence, like that of a Fra Angelico Madonna. *Since that time at your parents' I've been thinking things over* . . . They had spent Christmas with her parents in Rochester. It had not been a success. The house had been filled with what seemed like a constant stream of relatives and friends. She'd hardly spent any time alone with Saul. It had been as bad when they got back to their apartment. Saul had seemed moody and withdrawn, preferring the company of his college friends to hers – or so it seemed.

I know we were both upset and I'm sorry for some of the things I said that night . . . ('You've never loved me. You were just using me to get away from your parents,' he'd hissed. They had been arguing in whispers. The walls in her parents' house were thin.) . . . *but I think you were absolutely right when you said it was ridiculous to go on living apart like this and still expect to have some kind of meaningful relationship. Marriage is about commitment, right?*

Virginia's stomach, already in a delicate condition, gave a lurch as the plane descended through banks of swirling cloud. Through the scratched plastic porthole she could discern the vague outlines of green fields, dark shapes which might have been mountains or forest, networks of roads or rivers.

Commitment. It was a solid word, with a sound like the click of a key in a lock. Virginia yawned. The feeling of nausea was intensified by the drumming in her ears. She tried to swallow, but could not dispel the sensation of pressure. Certain phrases in the letter repeated themselves in her mind. After the bit about commitment, Saul had alluded to open marriages (*after all, we're mature adults* . . .), the unfairness of expecting absolute fidelity (*unrealistic, nowadays* . . .), the need for trust (*I think we need to be totally honest* . . .). She thought about her marriage, averting her mind from the possibility of catastrophe, as the plane banked and circled, awaiting permission to land.

They were the perfect couple. Or so their friends said. He was smart and she was pretty. How could they lose?

It became a matter for amicable dispute in the early days of their marriage as to which of them had seen the other first. Virginia, teasing, insisted she'd made the first move. Hadn't she asked for the loan of Saul's lecture notes on *Pride and Prejudice* that day in the English faculty library, their first semester at NYU? If she'd left it up to him to approach her, she'd have waited forever. Saul said that, on the contrary, he'd been watching her for weeks, nerving himself to speak to her. Whatever the truth of the matter, things had progressed fast enough after that. Although it wasn't until several weeks later, when he'd cast her as Ophelia to his Hamlet in the production he'd been directing for the Shakespeare Society, that they'd become lovers.

> My lord, I have remembrances of yours
> That I have longed long to re-deliver . . .

The production had been a success. He had sent her flowers on the first night, with a note: *Sweets to the sweet*. Her eyes filled with tears. How happy they'd been.

Marriage had not seemed that big an issue until towards the end of their final year. Until that point their little world of lectures and parties and amateur dramatics had seemed inviolable, existing within the charmed circle of academic life. Then suddenly, Virginia perceived, it was all coming to an end. A larger, colder world of responsibilities loomed. People were leaving, to get jobs or take up research places elsewhere. Couples who had seemed as good as married were drifting apart. It seemed inevitable that the same thing should happen to her and Saul.

Calling round at her room, a few days before the start of their final examinations, Saul found her in tears. When he tried to comfort her, she turned on him angrily. It was all right for him, the star student – he was bound to pass. There was a good chance she would fail. Then what would happen? He would leave her for that philosophy student with the big ass he'd found so fascinating at the *Twelfth Night* party. Denying this allegation, which was not unfounded, Saul had an intimation that more was at stake than wounded vanity. Clearly, something was expected of him. Over the next few days he began to understand what it was.

Living together was out of the question, Virginia said. Her parents would never permit it. And trial marriages never worked. You had to have a real commitment. That was the whole point. If you loved someone enough you wanted to be with them, didn't you? Maybe he didn't love her enough. Maybe he'd never loved her.

79

There had been a succession of conversations on the same theme. Resolved, on each occasion, in bed. Of course he loved her, he said. Further than that he was not prepared to go. The day of his final exam, they went out to eat. He ordered champagne and they both got slightly drunk. She remembered what happened next as if it were yesterday, instead of two years ago.

'What makes you think I don't want to get married?' he'd said.

All their friends came to the wedding. Saul's professor brought his wife along. Even Saul's parents showed up, his mother driving down from Vermont with his stepfather and the kids, his father flying in from LA with his new girlfriend. Virginia's father was well enough after his bypass surgery to give her away. She wore white lace and satin. It was everything she'd dreamed. A perfect day. They had spent their honeymoon at Cape Cod – Europe would have to wait till next year, Saul said – returning in September to look for a place to live.

The apartment they found in the West Village was small, but close enough to the University Library for Saul to go in every day. He'd started his postgraduate research at NYU, supervised by his old professor. Every day, after breakfasting with his wife, he caught the bus to Washington Square to work on the outline for his doctoral thesis. After washing the dishes and cleaning the apartment, Virginia too settled down to work. She was re-taking her math paper, in order to secure a place at a teacher training college the following year.

For the next six months everything went smoothly. Virginia adapted to the demands of her new life – cooking, cleaning, taking clothes to the laundromat, picking up groceries – with a pleased sense of her own competence. She did well in her math exam and was accepted for the teaching course she wanted. In two, maybe three years' time, she calculated, when Saul had got his doctorate and they'd saved enough money from her earnings, they could think about buying a place of their own. Later, when Saul had a job in a university somewhere, they'd start a family.

She'd been so preoccupied with these plans she never thought that Saul might have plans of his own, until the day he came in from work with the news that he'd been offered a place to do postgraduate research in Renaissance Literature at the University of Edinburgh.

'Oh, *Saul*. Why didn't you tell me?'

'I did tell you. We discussed all this weeks ago. That conversation I had with Mark – remember?'

'You said he thought you should go to Europe sometime. I didn't realize it was all fixed up.'

'What's the matter? Aren't you pleased? I thought you wanted to see Europe.'

'I am pleased. And I want to go. But . . . what about my course?'

'Forget your course. This is a great opportunity.'

'For you, maybe.'

It was their first real quarrel. When it was over, things had been said on both sides which could never be unsaid. His attitude was irresponsible, she said. If she passed up the chance to do the course this year, then it would be another full year before she could apply. She might not get accepted so easily. Then she could forget about getting a job, forget about the plans they had made. He said she made too many plans. She accused him of undervaluing her achievements. He denied it. She told him he didn't care about their future. He said if she hadn't been in such a hurry to get married, they wouldn't have to worry about the future. She called him selfish. He said she was over-reacting. All these allegations contained too much truth not to hurt intensely.

After they'd made it up, a coolness persisted. The issue had shifted from being a matter of expediency to being a question of pride. The future of their marriage seemed to turn on the capitulation of one to the wishes of the other. Neither side would surrender, each feeling too much was at stake. For

Saul, it was the academic achievement he'd worked for over the past four years; for Virginia, it was economic independence to be followed, in time, by domestic security.

In the end, a compromise was reached. Both would pursue their studies as planned. It was agreed that Virginia, whose course finished the following summer, would put off looking for a job for another year after she qualified, in order to join Saul for the second year of his studies in Edinburgh. After all, once she had her diploma, he pointed out, she could get a job anytime. And it was only a year, she reminded him. A year would go very quickly if they were both working. They would spend every vacation together, he said. She could come to Europe in the spring. Just as they had planned.

Virginia wondered if, after all, it would have been a good idea to have called him. In her excitement last night, when the woman had called to say there was a seat available on standby, the idea of arriving unannounced had seemed a good one. She would surprise him. Saul loved surprises. It would be the prelude to the greater surprise she had in store. Only now was she starting to regret her impulsiveness.

She yawned again, swallowing convulsively to dispel the bursting sensation in her eardrums. Another few minutes and they would be landing. Idly, as a way of distracting herself from the twin emotions of fear and uncertainty about the future which formed a tight knot in her stomach, she began to leaf through the magazine on her lap, feeling the slither of its high-gloss pages beneath her fingers. *Is There Life After Divorce? Do Men Want To Be Sex Objects?* A snarling blonde in a red silk flying-suit – *Baby, You've Come a Long, Long Way*.

The warning light came on. She flipped the magazine shut. Whatever happens, she thought, a shade despairingly, it's too late to turn back.

At the Arrivals gate she wasted no time in looking for a familiar face. After a brief, businesslike visit to the Ladies' room, where she vomited neatly into the sink, afterwards wiping her streaming eyes and nose with brusque efficiency, she felt better. She collected her luggage from the carousel and went in search of a cab. Her consciousness was in that state of near-suspension she was always able to attain whenever she had anything difficult to accomplish.

As the taxi reached the outskirts of the city she began to look about her, in the hope of seeing something – some landmark or familiar place-name – which would connect with the picture she'd already formed in her mind; a composite of things she'd read and remarks gleaned from Saul's letters. Wasn't there supposed to be a castle somewhere? All that could be seen from the moving car were drab concrete buildings resembling the housing projects back home, surrounded by bleak stretches of wasteground. Later there were streets of tiny suburban houses with front gardens. As they drew nearer to the centre of the city, the houses began to look more like the kind of thing she expected. They were miniature castles, adorned with turrets, crenellations, spires. Many of them bore a neon scribble. *Rooms Vacant. Car Park. Facilities.*

Her initial disappointment was succeeded by a shock of recognition – of relief, almost – as they entered Princes Street.

'Oh, look,' she cried. 'There it is. The castle.'

'Ay, it's still there.' The driver was watching the traffic. 'Now where was it you said?'

In the slanting light of early evening the tall stone houses in the New Town seemed to have no more solidity than structures of wood and canvas. As the cab nosed its way along the wide streets with their oddly familiar grid pattern, Virginia began to regret, for a panicky moment or two, her coming. The vague anxiety which had possessed her since the arrival of Saul's letter two days before, the exhausting flight with its hours-long wait between planes, its inedible meals offered at strange times, all combined to make her feel the uncertainty of her position. She felt a powerful impulse to turn back.

'Here we are.' The car pulled up in front of a row of

blackened stone houses, with steps leading up to each door. She was reminded of a dolls house she had once owned; the front lifted off and you could see all the rooms behind. She paid the driver and took her suitcase from the trunk. In the shadow of the tenement buildings the street was a gloomy channel, along which the wind swept pieces of torn paper, dust and human figures with equal indifference.

She climbed the stairs, rang the bell. After a moment the door was opened by a girl in jeans and a dirty sweater. Red lipstick.

'Yes?'

'I'm looking for Saul. Is he in?' Out of breath from climbing the stairs, Virginia felt a spasm of dizziness. When she opened her eyes the other woman was frowning at her.

'Are you feeling okay?'

'I'm fine. Is he in? I was going to phone him from the airport but then I thought, what the hell. Surprise him.'

'I'm sure you will,' the other murmured. 'Why don't you come in? Saul won't be long.'

'Oh, is he out?' She was unable to keep the tremor of disappointment out of her voice. 'I guess I should introduce myself. I'm Virginia – Saul's wife.'

'I rather thought you might be. I should leave your suitcase there. Would you like some tea?'

'I'd love some tea.' Virginia managed a smile. 'You must be Liz. Saul's told me so much about you . . .'

'Actually, I'm Catherine. Liz should be in soon.' She opened a door and stood aside for Virginia to pass. 'You can wait in here if you like.'

'My, what a lovely room.' Virginia subsided gratefully onto the shabby sofa, with its faded pattern of tropical birds. Despite the grandeur of its proportions, the room had a neglected look. There was dust on the big mirror over the fireplace, brittle everlasting flowers in a cracked jug, a pile of old newspapers cascading onto the floor.

'Yes, isn't it.' Catherine knelt to set a match to the gas-fire.

'Bit of a mess though.' She did not sound unduly perturbed by the admission. She stood up, brushing dust off the knees of her jeans. She had a nice figure, Virginia observed. Her face was pretty, in a sullen kind of way. But her hair looked as if it needed a wash.

'Milk and sugar?' she said.

'Pardon me? Oh. Yes, please. One and a half spoonfuls. When did you move in?'

'Oh, a while ago.'

'Only Saul didn't mention there was someone else living here . . .'

'Forgetful of him.'

'That's what confused me. The names . . .'

'Don't give it another thought. I'll close the door if you don't mind,' Catherine said, 'only there's a bit of a draught in here.'

'Go ahead.' Virginia felt hungover with fatigue. She closed her eyes for a second and when she opened them again the room was empty. Suspended between waking and sleeping, between familiar and unfamiliar realities, she wondered if perhaps she hadn't dreamed the whole thing – the flight, the drive, her conversation with the girl – and if she wasn't, after all, about to wake with a stiff neck and the beginnings of a headache in the living room back home.

Her gaze moved around the room in which she now found herself, touching on objects: a fine mirror; an ugly lamp; some taxidermist's nightmare in a glass case; a faded daguerrotype of the Parthenon. Each perceived with the rapt intensity of things seen in a dream.

The faint percussion of porcelain on porcelain startled her awake. Catherine was handing her a cup of tea. She had the odd sensation, as she took it, that the other had been watching her as she slept.

'Thank you.' She struggled to sit upright against the collapsing sofa cushions. Her throat felt dry and she drank the cooling tea with hasty greed.

'You should lie down for a while. You look exhausted. Was it a long flight?'

'Not too bad.' She held out her cup for a refill, noticing with distaste that the rim was chipped. 'I'll be okay for a while. He'll be back soon, won't he?'

'I expect so.'

'What time is it?' She could not have said what it was exactly, but something about the way the other woman was looking at her made Virginia nervous.

'Six.'

The front door slammed. Both women glanced towards the sound. Neither spoke. Virginia ran her fingers through her hair, fluffing up its dark curls. No time to repair her make-up. The door opened and a tall woman dressed like a highwayman in a black cape and boots came in.

'Hello Liz,' said Catherine, and then with a certain formality, 'this is Virginia. Saul's wife.'

'Hi,' said Virginia.

'Well,' said the tall woman, unwinding what seemed to Virginia to be an inordinate length of woollen scarf. 'Gosh. Hello. When did you arrive?'

'Half an hour ago?' She looked at Catherine for confirmation. The other nodded. 'Cathy let me in.'

'That was a bit of luck. Her being here, I mean.' Liz divested herself of shawls, gloves, sweaters. 'Saul didn't mention you were coming . . .'

'He doesn't know yet,' Virginia said, a shade defensively. Suddenly her impetuous decision had acquired an aura of recklessness. 'It was meant to be a surprise.'

'I'll say,' said Liz, glancing at Catherine, who frowned slightly. 'Is there any more tea in the pot or shall I make a fresh one?'

'I'll do it.' Catherine got up. Almost in the same moment, there was the sound of a key in the lock.

'Ah,' said Liz. 'The moment of truth.'

★

Five forty-five. Saul replaced the top on his fountain pen and stacked the papers on the desk in front of him into a neat pile. He yawned and stretched, scraping his chair noisily on the marble floor of the Reading Room as he did so. Across the aisle, a middle-aged woman who had been making notes with furious concentration glanced up, frowning. He caught her eye and grinned.

He was feeling pleased with himself and with the world. He felt he had a lot to be pleased about. He was young, he was healthy, he was loved by two women. He'd done a good day's work and was looking forward to an evening's pleasure.

It was Catherine's birthday. He was taking her out to dinner, then to a late-night screening of *Hiroshima, Mon Amour*. He'd seen it once before, at a student film club, and wondered if it would seem as good the second time around. The opening sequence in which the camera slowly travelled over the lovers' entwined bodies had aroused and disturbed him, he recalled. Smooth limbs seen in close-up intercut with images of the shattered city.

He sauntered across to where she had been sitting, on the far side of the stacks. The place was empty. Only a pile of reserved books and a half page of indecipherable scrawl showed she had been there. He folded the piece of paper and put it in his pocket. His euphoria somewhat deflated, he stood irresolute in the middle of the floor, surrounded on all sides by the toiling figures of his fellow workers. Where the hell *was* she? He checked out his books at the desk and descended the stairs to the foyer, where the revolving doors drew him into their maelstrom and cast him out on the street.

He fell into the drifting crowd of late-night shoppers as into the currents of a stream and for a while felt himself carried along by its momentum. Faces came towards him out of the crowd but he did not see them, blind to all but his obsession. Last night he had drawn her onto him, penetrating her from behind so that she was unable to move; impaled, her spine arched back against his chest, her face averted. As he felt himself start to come he struggled to see her face, to glimpse there some reflection of his own desire in that human mirror. But she would not turn, preferring to be quite alone in her pleasure, as if he were no more than an instrument to gratify her perverse wish.

It was with an effort of will that he pulled himself out of the crowd, a tired swimmer making for the shore. He turned down Frederick Street, walking into the evening sun. For a minute or two he was blind. Alternate stripes of light and shadow thrown by the iron railings barred the pavement. The effect was stroboscopic, hallucinatory. He was aware of the distant buzz of traffic and of another sound, the murmur of his racing blood, which drummed in his ears like that of a diver about to break surface.

He had an intimation that something was different the minute he opened the door. It was an indefinable disturbance, like the evanescent trail left by a woman's perfume, or the silence which precedes the ringing of the telephone. Then he saw the suitcase with the PanAm stickers. Its twin was under the bed in his room. He read the name on the address label just to make sure. *Christ*.

He regarded the closed door of the living room with a feeling approaching dread. He became aware of the murmur of voices. Suddenly nervous, he put up his hand to smooth his hair and caught sight of his reflection in the hall-stand mirror. The silver had flaked off the back in places, leaving black spots which floated across his face like the marks of some disease. His eyes had a haunted look. He opened the door.

'When did *you* get here?' he said.

'Hi darling.' Virginia made a movement towards him. She was smiling, but he heard the tremor in her voice. 'Guess what? I just dropped in.'

'Why didn't you tell me you were coming?' He hoped the

dismay he was feeling was not too apparent. 'I could've met you at the airport.'

'I wanted it to be a surprise. Only you weren't in.'

'How was I supposed to know?' He sounded almost angry.

'Oh, it's okay,' she said, 'Cathy here let me in.' She reached up to embrace him. Through the hot tangle of her hair he was aware of the sardonic look on Catherine's face. 'Wasn't it lucky? I wasn't sure I'd come to the right address until I mentioned your name.'

There was a short silence.

'I'll make that tea,' said Liz.

A new and terrible thought occurred to Saul. The bedroom. He couldn't remember how he had left it when he went out that morning. Had he made the bed? And what about Catherine's things. The clothes she'd discarded the night before. Her lipstick on the bedside table.

'Aren't you going to take your coat off, honey?'

'Right away . . .' he said, backing out of the room. 'I'll just . . .'

In the bedroom he ripped the sheets from the bed and opened the window wide to expunge all traces of Catherine's scent from the atmosphere. There were some clothes on the chair. Without checking to see if any of his own things were amongst them, he bundled them into the room next door. On the floor by the bed was a crumpled Kleenex, blotted with a lipstick kiss. He thrust it into his pocket. Nothing else, thank God.

In the drawing room he had the impression he had walked onto an improvised set for *Three Sisters*: Olga and Irene chatting over the samovar. Masha at the window, waiting for her lover.

'Have some tea.' Virginia patted the vacant seat beside her. His pretty little wife, smiling up at him. 'You look tired. You haven't been working too hard, have you?'

'I feel fine.' He wished Catherine would sit down, instead of hanging around on the edge of the room like some vengeful

89

ghost. She was standing at the window, her arms clasped around herself. The narrow sliver of cheek and profile he could see made him shiver, recalling that apparition of the night. Her averted face. The long curve of her spine.

'You always work too hard. I was just saying to Cathy . . .'

'How was the flight?' he said, to distract her.

'Tiring.' She yawned, delicate as a cat. 'Maybe I will lie down for a spell.'

'I'll show you the room,' he said.

'Well,' Catherine said, 'this *is* a surprise.'

'Believe me – ' he realized he was whispering ' – I had no idea she was coming. This is as much a shock to me as it is to you.'

'I wouldn't call it a shock exactly. Although I have to admit when I opened the door and saw her standing there I felt a bit . . .'

'Look . . .'

'. . . nonplussed. Not shocked. And then of course as soon as she opened her mouth I knew who it was.'

'I'm sorry.'

'Don't be.' There was a new packet of cigarettes on the table. She stripped off the cellophane and began to play with it, winding it around her finger. 'She's very pretty,' she said. He ignored this remark.

'Where were you this afternoon? I looked for you in the library, but you'd left.'

'I wanted to wash my hair. We were supposed to be going out, remember?'

He could not stop himself glancing at the door.

'About tonight . . .' He was unable to keep the conspiratorial note from his voice. 'It looks like we'll have to change our plans.'

'It does, doesn't it?' She lit a cigarette. Her hand shook slightly.

★

He looked in on Virginia. She was asleep, lying on her side. A faint snoring sound came from her open mouth. Beneath the thin skin of her eyelids her eyes flickered in dreams.

At the foot of the bed was her suitcase, half-unpacked, an envelope lying on top. His own handwriting jumped out at him. That stupid letter. He recalled some of the things he had written. All that crap about being honest with her. Who was he trying to kid? If he was really honest, he would let her know the kind of man she was married to. Adulterer. Hypocrite.

He felt a rush of tenderness, of pity, towards the sleeping woman. On the wall above her head the print he disliked but had never got around to changing had been knocked out of true. *The Marriage of the Arnolfini.* The colour registration was poor. Colour from the bride's gown had bled into the flesh-tones, giving them a greenish tinge. The unblinking eye of the round mirror regarded him as, careful not to disturb his unconscious wife, he leaned across and straightened the picture.

I've got to get out of here.

In the street he breathed deeply, like a man released from prison. The smell of exhaust fumes hung in the air. A gritty wind stung his cheeks. How long he walked he could not afterwards recollect, or where his wanderings led him. The city was a desert of shifting surfaces; their apparent solidity a trick to confuse the unwary. As he walked between buildings coloured like smoke or sand, he planned what he would say to his wife.

Complete honesty, that was the thing. This time it could not be avoided. It was a pity she and Catherine had had to meet, but (he argued with himself, wandering in the labyrinth of interconnecting squares and circuses) it was her own fault. What had possessed her to arrive like this, without warning? Had she, perhaps, suspected his betrayal? Hoped to surprise him in the act? No, the thought was too fantastic.

Complete honesty. He would tell her tonight, over dinner.

★

When he returned Virginia was awake. She sat at the dressing-table, putting on make-up. She smiled at him in the mirror as she smoothed the ivory paste over her cheeks and forehead, her face, beneath this pale veneer, resembling an unfinished drawing.

'Hi darling,' she said. 'Where did you get to?'

'I went for a walk. You were asleep.'

'That's okay.' Sucking in her cheeks as if she had bitten into something sour she smeared twin arcs of rouge onto her cheekbones, blurring the hard lines with her fingertips. 'Cathy said you probably wouldn't be gone long.'

'Why didn't you let me know you were coming?'

She did not reply immediately, intent on her reflection. With an artist's steady hand she drew bold swathes of purple on each eyelid. 'Can we talk about it later?' Stretching her lips wide she pencilled a brown line around the outer edge. When it was perfect she coloured in the bare strip of flesh with crimson, serious as a child crayoning a picture.

'I just don't understand why you didn't write me. Or phone.'

Virginia covered the whole freshly painted image with fine white powder. For a second or two the colours grew dim, then glowed with febrile brilliance as she flicked away the dust. Her eyes were bright as she turned from the mirror to look at him. The small lines of fatigue he had noticed earlier had smoothed themselves out in sleep.

'Don't be angry,' she said. 'Aren't you going to kiss me?'

For a moment she seemed vulnerable as a child. He put his arms around her, smelling the sweet, powdery fragrance of her skin, familiar to him as his own smell.

'I missed you.'

'I missed you too.' Honesty would have to wait until it had had a few drinks to fortify it. 'Shall we go someplace and eat?'

'I thought you'd never ask.' She was already putting on her coat. She had lost weight, he noticed.

'I can't believe this place,' she whispered, clutching his arm

92

with nervous laughter as they descended the dark stairs. 'Isn't it *weird*? That room. All that junk. Stuffed birds and God knows what else . . .'

'You get used to it,' he said. 'After a while, you even start to like it.'

In the restaurant they sat surrounded by mirrors which threw back images of Virginia. These were multiplied by the reflecting surfaces of cutlery, wine glasses and by the copper tabletops which were a feature of the place. Another was its Art Nouveau stained glass, each window portraying scenes from Arthurian legend. After his second or third glass of wine, Saul felt he was looking at everything through a fiery mist. The fluttering movements of his wife's hands as they carried morsels of food to her lips struck him particularly. Her slender fingers with their glittering rings turning the wine glass round and round.

She talked of people they knew. Friends from NYU. Ellen, the girl she was sub-letting the apartment to. Her parents. Small sounds she made – her laugh, the flicking of her nails against the rim of the glass – grated on his nerves. *Complete honesty*. The trouble was, he had no idea how to begin. As he half listened, tuning in and out of his wife's conversation, his gaze fixed itself on the coloured glass panel behind her head, a representation of St George and the dragon. The mailed foot of the Red Cross Knight crushing the serpent's head, the writhing figure of the virgin captive, naked except for her coiling hair . . .

He considered ways of beginning, rejecting them all as too abrupt or too tentative. ('Virginia, we have to talk . . .'; 'Virginia, there's something I have to tell you . . .') As he hesitated between alternatives, he became aware that she was speaking.

'You haven't been listening to a word I've said.'

Her look was reproachful. With an effort of will he focused

his attention on her face, her hands. He wondered if she would cry. He didn't want her to cry.

'I'm sorry. Look, Virginia, I . . .'

'It's okay. It's just that you've been so quiet and . . . Oh Saul, I don't know how to say this . . . I mean, there's something I have to tell you.'

She had taken the words right out of his mouth. He stared at her.

'I'm pregnant.'

There was a pause.

'Are you sure?' he said.

'Of course I'm sure. You don't think I'd have come all this way if . . .' She looked at him. 'What's the matter? Aren't you pleased?'

'It's a bit of a shock, that's all.'

'As soon as I got the results of the test I called the travel agent. Luckily they had a few seats on standby, so I thought . . . Oh Saul, you are pleased, aren't you?'

'That means it's definite then?'

'What?'

'The test. You said you had a test. That means you're definitely . . .'

'Yes.'

'Fine.'

'You *are* upset. I was afraid you'd be upset. That's why I didn't want to tell you on the phone. I almost did, you know, just after I called the hospital. I had the phone in my hand and I was going to call you but then . . .'

'How did it happen?'

'I called the travel agent instead. What do you mean, how did it happen? The way it usually happens, I guess. You were there, weren't you?'

'Keep your voice down. What I meant was, we were so careful . . .'

'You're forgetting that time at my parents'. At New Year.'

'Oh my God. But didn't you . . .'

94

'No I didn't. You said it didn't matter.'

'I don't remember saying that.'

'You did. We were lying in bed and you distinctly said . . .'

'Just keep your voice down, will you? People are staring.'

'I don't care. I came all this way to tell you and all you can say is . . .'

'Don't get upset. For God's sake. Please don't cry.'

'. . . why weren't we more careful, as if it was *my* fault or something.'

'What I meant was, I thought we'd agreed . . . Oh forget it.'

'Agreed what? You said you wanted children.'

'I said eventually. When I'd finished my thesis. When we'd got a place to live. When I'd found a job. What about your course? I thought it was so important to you.'

'It was. It is. Only I don't know what I want, anymore . . .'

'Don't cry. Baby, *please* . . .'

'I'm sorry. I'm just tired I guess. I was so excited when I found out about the baby. I wanted to tell you right away. I guess I just didn't think.'

'It doesn't matter. We'll work something out. How many weeks along are you?'

'About twelve, I think. I worked it out on a chart.'

'That's not very far. Is it?'

'What are you talking about?'

'I mean . . . It's not too far . . . If you decided . . . Well, you know . . .'

'I have decided.' Her face was stony, her lips compressed. Eyes downcast like those of a carved saint on a monument. An expression he had once loved, until he realised it made her resemble her mother. For a while they sat not looking at each other as waves of noise broke around them. Laughter. The clatter of knives and forks.

'I'm sorry,' he said at last. She flinched, as if the sound of his voice were more than she could bear.

'I thought you'd be pleased. I really thought you'd be

pleased.' Her voice was a shaky whisper. Her eyes brimmed with tears.

'I *am* pleased. It just takes a little getting used to.'

'You said you wanted us to have babies. Someday.'

Babies! Her disingenuous use of the plural appalled him. He didn't trust himself to speak. Unable to meet her gaze, he studied the crumbs on the tablecloth, the oyster shells on their layer of melting ice.

'I know it's sooner than we intended, but . . .'

Their little drama was attracting curious glances. A waiter hovered within earshot.

'Do you want anything else? Some dessert maybe? Some coffee?' He was hoping she would refuse so they could get the check and go.

She shook her head. 'I don't want any dessert. And coffee gives me the most terrible heartburn. Maybe a glass of water . . .'

'Can we have a glass of water please?' Why didn't she just announce it to the whole room? I'm pregnant, coffee gives me heartburn, my husband just asked me to have an abortion.

'I'll call a taxi,' he said.

6

For the next two days Catherine's exchanges with her lover were of the briefest kind. He had returned one of her lipsticks to her, under cover of borrowing a book, and had elicited from her the opening times of the National Gallery. Recovered from her transatlantic crossing, Virginia wanted to be shown the city about which Saul had told her so much.

Catherine herself had spent most of the weekend in the faculty library and it was there, on the deserted fourth floor of the building, amongst the stacks of unread books and unreadable theses, that Saul found her.

'Hi.'

She glanced up from the book she had been reading, or trying to read. 'Oh, hello.'

There was a silence which both seemed disinclined to break.

'I guess you must be pretty angry,' he said at last.

'Don't be silly.'

'Not that I'd blame you if you were.'

'Why should I be angry? It was inevitable something like this would happen. We both knew that.'

'For the past couple of days I've been in a state of shock, you know? Like every morning I wake up and I can't believe it's really happening . . .'

'I know what you mean.'

'I keep thinking what a fool I've been. If I'd just had the nerve to *tell* her . . .'

'It's too late to think about that now.'

'I guess you're right.' He was silent a minute, lost in his own thoughts.

'I've got to go,' said Catherine. 'I'm seeing Hobson at ten. Why don't we meet for lunch?'

'I can't,' he said dejectedly. 'I said I'd have lunch with Virginia. I'm supposed to be showing her round the university. She wants to see where I work. Meet all the friends I've told her so much about . . .' He covered his face with his hands, a gesture which struck her as a shade histrionic.

'It's not that important,' she said. 'We can do it some other time.'

'You don't understand. It's worse that that.' He raised despairing eyes. 'She's pregnant.'

There was a brief pause.

'I suppose that does make things more interesting,' said Catherine.

After the initial shock of meeting her lover's wife, Catherine soon got used to having her around. Her presence in the flat was not, in any case, one that could easily be ignored. Traces of her personality pervaded the atmosphere: the bathroom was full of her lotions and powders, her pale pink monogrammed towels; brassieres and pantihose, hung from the drying racks in the kitchen, filled the air with their faint perfume. To the stacks of ageing newspapers and issues of the *New Statesman* in the living room were added shiny copies of *Vogue* and *Cosmopolitan*.

Within a few days of her arrival the flat seemed transformed. Everything sparkled with unnatural radiance. Windowpanes shone, furniture gleamed. Even the dusty mausoleum where the snake eternally brooded on his revenge glowed dully beneath Virginia's housewifely ministrations.

'What else should I do all day – sit around?' she said when reproached for excessive zeal. 'You people have to work. Besides, I enjoy it, really.'

Cooking was something else she enjoyed apparently. Catherine would return from the library at six to the smell of roasting meat, aromatic stews, baking bread. On some days the place smelled like a bakery. Quiches, croissants and waffles appeared on the scoured pine table, delicate flakes and crumbs scattering on Virginia's freshly washed floor.

She seemed consumed by restless energy; as if, Catherine thought, she were making up for lost time. Or trying to justify her existence.

One Sunday, a week after Virginia's arrival, Catherine rose late from her narrow bed to find the others having breakfast. The air was heavy with the smell of baking mingled with a certain tension. A quarrel in the making.

'Hi Cathy,' said Virginia. 'Want some coffee?'

'Try one of these croissants,' said Guy, his mouth full. 'They're delicious.'

'I'm sure Cathy wants to come along.' Virginia handed her the coffee. 'Don't you, Cathy?'

'Where?' She yawned and blinked, conscious of her sour mouth and of an incipient headache.

'You look a bit rough,' said Liz.

'I feel it.' Over the litter of Sunday newspapers and breakfast dishes her eyes met Saul's for a guilty second. He looked away.

'We're all going to Holyrood House,' said Virginia. 'Only Saul doesn't want to come . . .'

'I have a paper to finish.' In the monogrammed towelling dressing-gown Virginia had bought him, his hair combed back in two wet wings over his ears, a dab of congealed blood on his chin where he had cut himself shaving, he looked, Catherine thought, the very picture of an unhappily married man.

'You need a break. You've been working all week. Sunday is a day of rest,' said Virginia, with the happy air of someone discovering a truth in cliché.

'Not in my religion,' he muttered, smashing a croissant to airy fragments.

★

Built of pale yellow stone, Holyrood House resembled a toy castle. Beyond it, in the cultivated wilderness of Holyrood Park, crouched the massive leonine shape of the extinct volcano. As they crossed the wide forecourt Catherine felt the cold spring sunshine pierce the fog of her hangover. Sounds seemed crystalline, sharp. The world sparkled with painful radiance.

'Oh darling, isn't it pretty?' said Virginia. 'Like something out of a fairytale.'

Saul, who had capitulated to his wife's wishes with a bad grace, made a non-committal sound.

'The history's actually rather grim,' said Liz, who was acting as guide. 'But then so are most fairytales. Shall we go inside?'

They climbed the Great Staircase, Liz and Guy taking it in turns to point out interesting features to Virginia. Saul and Catherine fell into step behind. On the walls tapestries depicted lovers in a formal garden, embracing amongst groves of orange trees.

'Why are you avoiding me?' He had paused, ostensibly to examine a series of paintings on the first-floor landing, depicting scenes from classical myth. *The Rape of Europa. Cupid and Psyche.*

'I'm not. It's just a very difficult situation.'

'You're telling me. What are we going to do, for God's sake?'

'There's nothing we can do.'

They followed the others into a room hung with more tapestries. These had faded, in the strong light, to a bluish monochrome. The theme, appropriate to a bedchamber, was love in various manifestations: Jove appearing to Danae as a shower of gold; Leda spreading her legs to the swan.

'What bizarre tastes they had in the sixteenth century.'

'Catherine, I have to talk to you . . .'

'I'm listening.'

'Not here,' he said. 'Not now . . .'

100

A party of French tourists approaching from the opposite direction cut them off, temporarily, from the others. Saul caught her by the wrist. 'Wait. What about tomorrow? I'll meet you.'

'Alright. Now let go.'

The tour guide was giving an animated account of the events which had taken place in the room in which they were standing on 9 March 1566. A private supper party. A few close friends of the queen. Rizzio, her favourite, rumoured to be the father of her child. An evening of music, followed by a game of cards.

'You know I'm crazy about you, don't you?'

Catherine was looking at a portrait of a glowering dark young man in sixteenth-century dress. His lips, below the thin moustache, were voluptuous as a girl's. A single pearl drop hung from his earlobe.

'I even dreamed about you last night . . .'

The guide had reached the climax of his narrative. The murderers bursting into the chamber. Cards scattering: king, queen, knave. Weapons flashing.

'*Riccio, bien sûr terrifié, s'est accroché aux jupes de Marie, en l'implorant d'un air pitoyable "Sauvez ma vie, madame, sauvez ma vie . . ."*'

'Then I hope you don't talk in your sleep.'

They turned the corner and walked into Virginia, descending the spiral staircase down which the corpse of the little singing master had tumbled in its last headlong flight.

'There you are,' she said. 'I was wondering where you'd got to.'

'We got stranded by a bunch of French tourists,' said Saul. 'We had the murder of Rizzio in two languages.'

'It's so romantic isn't it?'

'Sex and death,' said Saul. 'I guess it is pretty romantic.'

Liz and Guy were in the picture gallery. Portraits of one hundred and eleven Scottish kings and queens were set into the panelling.

'It says here,' Liz was referring to her guidebook, 'that these were painted by someone called De Wit. James VII's court painter. Apparently, most of them never existed.'

'Imaginary kings,' said Guy. 'Interesting concept. Still, what's a couple of dozen ancestors more or less? Do you suppose he got paid by the yard?'

'Either that, or he was faced with summary execution if he failed to make his quota.'

'I have to sit down for a minute,' Virginia said abruptly.

'Are you feeling okay, sweetheart?'

'I'm fine. Just tired.' ·

'Why didn't you say so before?' He put his arm round her. 'You have to take care of yourself you know . . .'

'I told you, I'm absolutely fine.' Virginia seemed not displeased by the attention however. 'You worry too much.'

'There's a chair over there. By the door,' said Guy.

Catherine watched as Virginia, supported by the two men, crossed the gleaming expanse of polished floorboards. A cold light fell through the tall windows which formed one side of the ornate room, in which kings and queens, imaginary or otherwise, had once passed the time of day. She caught Liz's eye.

'It must have been awful for you these last few days,' said Liz.

'It hasn't been easy.'

'Saul said she might be staying for a while,' Liz said, a shade apologetically. 'I mean, he asked me if it was okay. I didn't see how I could refuse under the circumstances.' She hesitated a moment. 'I suppose he's told you she's pregnant?'

'Yes. Perfect timing, isn't it?'

'That's one way of looking it,' said Liz, as they went to join the waiting group at the exit.

As Catherine crossed North Bridge Street on her way up to the university, a girl in tartan bondage trousers and a black T-shirt inscribed with the word *DESTROY* asked her for a light, then ambled off with her companions. Catherine watched their stately progress along the street. Pale warriors. 'I think the end of the world is at hand,' she said to Saul in the subterranean tea-room of the University Library.

He was drawing patterns on the table-top with a spent match. Intricate designs of spilled coffee and ash. Spirals, sunbursts. He looked up. 'If you mean things are in a mess, I couldn't agree more. What are we going to do?'

'I thought we'd discussed that.'

'So what did we decide? It seems to have slipped my mind. Oh, sure, I remember now. We should act like nothing happened, right?'

'I didn't say that.'

'Let me tell you what I think. I think we need to decide what we want. I know what I want. How about you?'

Before she could reply they were joined by Robin Orr, carrying a plate of lasagne. 'I hear you've got a visitor,' he said to Saul.

'Who told you that?'

'A little bird. Name of Magda,' said Robin through a forkful of pasta. 'It must make things rather complicated for you . . .'

'Things are just fine,' said Saul. 'We really should be going,' he said to Catherine.

'I hope you haven't forgotten about Sunday week,' Robin said, also addressing Catherine.

Caught in the crossfire, she thought.

'Gilly's birthday. Eight o'clock.' He looked at Saul. 'Why don't you join us? Bring your wife, if you like.'

'Thanks.'

'I'll tell Gilly to expect an extra couple for dinner,' said Robin. There was an edge of malice to his smile. 'I'm afraid that'll make us an odd number though. We'll have to see if we can find you a spare man,' he said to Catherine.

'That bastard,' Saul said furiously when they were outside. 'I guess that's his idea of a joke.'

'It's just his manner. You shouldn't let that kind of thing get to you.'

'I don't understand you people,' he said. 'I never know when you're being serious.'

'Oh, people like Robin make a point of not being serious about anything. It would spoil their self-image.'

'I wasn't talking about Robin,' he said morosely.

In the little park at the centre of George Square the chestnut trees were in leaf. There were snowdrops, aconites. A fresh, cold smell. The only sounds the metallic rustle of birdsong and the crunch of footsteps on the gravel.

'I suppose this means the end of a beautiful friendship,' Catherine said, after they had been walking for a while in silence.

'What are you talking about?'

'Isn't it obvious? I really don't see how we can go on. Not now.'

'That lets us both off the hook, doesn't it?' The bitterness with which he spoke surprised her.

'Oh, come on. I can hardly go on sleeping with you while your wife's around. Unless you think she wouldn't mind . . .' The exasperation she felt at his intransigence was coloured by another feeling. Curiosity, perhaps. The desire to see what he would do next, how readily, if it came to that, he would relinquish her.

'I never suggested that. It seems to me you're in kind of a hurry to say it's all over. I mean, you haven't even considered the alternatives.'

'What *are* the alternatives?'

'Maybe you want it to be over. I guess that's it. Maybe you don't care about me enough.'

She made a gesture of impatience. 'That's got nothing to do with it.'

'Hasn't it?'

Catherine was silent. And yet she knew there was something in what he said. Her affectlessness was one of her least admirable qualities. Looked at in a certain light it was nothing more than coldness. A refusal to get involved. At moments like these it was as if she were watching the scene from a distance; as if the protagonists, of which she herself was one, were characters in some poorly scripted film.

'So tell me,' he said. 'I can take it.'

'I don't like declarations. Or ultimatums. You know that.'

At the centre of the park where the paths converged was a bench. They sat down, a little apart. After a few minutes Saul touched Catherine's hand. 'You're cold,' he said. He took her hands and put them inside his coat to warm them.

She spread her fingers against his chest, feeling the beating heart beneath the bone. 'I'm sorry,' she said.

'It doesn't matter. Maybe you're right. We should stop this.'

'I don't want to.'

'Listen,' he said, 'I ran into Stuart this morning – you know, that guy I used to room with? He's going to France for a month at Easter. He said we could use his room while he's away. What do you think?'

'I hadn't realized you were capable of such duplicity.'

'That shows how little you know me,' said Saul, with the ghost of a smile.

The resentment which Saul had been feeling towards his wife was dispelled by the realization that her presence, although introducing a complication, did not mean the end of his affair. If his encounters with Catherine were less frequent and took place in uncomfortable and occasionally squalid surroundings, they were heightened by a sense of the clandestine. He'd never had such great sex.

Towards his wife he was more affectionate; given permission, he almost felt, by his lover's professed indifference. After all, Virginia was still his wife. He still loved her, in a funny kind of way. And although he was unfaithful, he was not wholly unfeeling. So he made efforts to keep Virginia happy. Made love to her more often. Brought her flowers on her birthday.

He blamed himself for the situation, of course. If he'd only spoken out in time – told her he'd fallen in love with another woman, that there was no future in staying together – all this might have been prevented. As it was, there was the child – a hostage to fortune. In that, at least, she was to blame, he felt.

7

At a little after eight on a fine April evening, at the beginning of what would turn out to be an unusually good summer, Catherine crossed the bridge over the Water of Leith into Dean Village. She was wearing a new dress and carried a bottle of wine in one hand and the poems of Andrew Marvell, a gift for Gillian, in the other. A few streets further on she turned off. It was here, on the first floor of a Victorian terraced house converted into flats, that the Orrs lived, with their cat, their books, their record collection and their portable typewriters.

Gillian opened the door. Her pale face beneath the straight dark fringe was untouched by make-up. She wore a white blouse, ruffled at the throat and wrists in a style reminiscent of the English Civil War. The two women kissed.

'How lovely. You shouldn't have.' Gillian unwrapped her gift. 'Look, Rob, one of your favourites.'

'Oh, absolutely.' Robin uncorked a bottle of wine. 'Worms and virginity. Delightfully morbid. Red? White?'

'Red please. Hello, Virginia.'

'Hi, Cathy. I love your dress. Don't you love her dress, Saul?'

'Oh, sure.'

He and Virginia were dressed as if for some more formal occasion, Saul in a dark suit, his wife in a silk shirtwaist dress, its elegant lines distended somewhat by her now visible pregnancy.

'We were just saying how nice it is to get out once in a while,' she said. 'Saul and I don't go out much these days, do we, darling? I'm always tired and he's always working late at the library . . .'

'Is he really? How impressive.' Robin returned with some glasses. 'Gilly and I almost never work in the library. It's so much nicer at home, we feel.'

'That's what I try and tell my husband,' said Virginia with a touch of petulance, 'but he says he can't concentrate with me around . . .'

'There are books I need to consult. Manuscripts,' said Saul.

'Ah, of course.' There was the faintest note of incredulity in Robin's voice. 'Manuscripts.'

'I don't see why you can't borrow them,' Virginia objected. 'I thought that was the whole idea of libraries.'

'Excuse me.' Robin went to answer the door.

'Do we have to discuss this now?' said Saul.

'Not if it upsets you, darling.' Virginia examined a piece of china, part of Gillian's collection of Clarice Cliff, picked up, Gillian was in the habit of explaining, for next to nothing. 'What a cute room. So much nicer than ours, Saul. Look at all these old books.' She ran her fingers along the spines of Robin's collection of thirties first editions.

Saul met Catherine's eyes. *Help me out, for God's sake*, the look said. It was the first social occasion he had attended since his wife's arrival. He hadn't wanted to go, but Virginia had insisted. 'How's your thesis going?' he said to Catherine after a pause.

'Fine. How's yours?'

'Oh fine. Just fine.' Another pause.

'Can't you two find anything else to talk about?' said Virginia.

Robin returned with Jonathan Strange, whom Catherine had known slightly at Cambridge and with whom, once or twice since they had met in Edinburgh, she had been invited to tea, a ceremonial occasion involving a choice of Indian or China, cucumber sandwiches and two kinds of cake. His unashamed enjoyment of such anachronisms was one of the things she liked about him. This evening, as on the previous occasions she had met him, he was dressed with a formality in which there was an element of self-parody.

'Hello darling.' He kissed her lightly on the lips.

'Do you know Saul?' said Robin. 'Saul Meyer, Jonathan Strange.'

'I've heard a lot about you,' Jonathan said, looking at Catherine.

'This is Virginia. My wife,' said Saul. There was a barely perceptible pause.

'Well,' Jonathan took Virginia's hand in his. 'How delightful to meet you at last.'

'I hope you're not going to talk about your research all night,' she said, smiling up at him and shaking her dark curls.

'God forbid,' he murmured. 'I never talk about work if I can help it.'

'What a relief. Saul never stops. He and Catherine are always comparing notes on something or other, aren't you, darling?' said Virginia.

'How *tiresome* of them.'

'I'm sure they don't intend to exclude me from the conversation. But that's the effect it has.'

'Oh, we're all guilty of it, to an extent,' said Gillian airily. 'It's all terribly incestuous. I mean, all one's friends are doing research, so one ends up eating it, sleeping it . . .'

'Or sleeping *with* it,' murmured Jonathan.

Catherine felt a bubble of nervous laughter rise in her throat. She didn't dare to look at Saul. The expression of studied unconcern she knew she would see on his face would have been too much for her. It was funny the way her friends brought out the worst in each other, she thought.

'I'll just . . . ah . . .' Gillian withdrew to the safety of the kitchen. 'Help yourselves to drinks,' she called over her shoulder.

'How long are you staying?' Jonathan offered to refill Virginia's glass. She refused with a little shake of the head.

'I don't know.' She shot a demure, sidelong look at her husband. 'That depends on Saul.'

'I can see that it might.' He poured himself a glass of wine, sniffed at it, made a face and drank. 'So what do you think of Edinburgh?'

'It's just fascinating. So historic. Ancient ruins everywhere you look . . .'

'Most of them in the English department,' muttered Robin, squatting in front of his record collection. 'Now, where did I put it?'

'It's like every time you walk down the street you step straight into the past,' said Virginia. 'We just don't have anything like it back home.'

'How wonderful. A country without a past.'

'I didn't see you in the library this afternoon,' Saul said to Catherine.

'I had a drink with Magda at lunchtime. Then I went home and fell asleep.'

'I hope Magda hasn't forgotten about tonight,' said Gillian. Did she say she might be late?'

'No. She did say she was meeting Donald though.'

'Is that the rather alarming chap with the red hair and the impenetrable accent?' Jonathan said. 'Where on earth did Magda find him? In the Clydeside shipyards, one imagines.'

'Actually he's a writer,' Gillian said reprovingly. 'Quite a good one, apparently. Or so Magda says.'

'What kind of things does he write?' said Saul. It explained a lot, he thought. The red-haired guy's aggressive attitude, his sleazy appearance. A typical writer.

Gillian shrugged. 'Novels. Gritty social realism. Not that I've ever read a word he's written, but . . .'

'One can tell just by looking at him the kind of thing he'd write,' said Robin. 'My Struggle. Confessions of a Working-Class Hero. Reading Proust in the outside lavvy and screwing the boss's daughter.'

'Don't say that to Magda,' said Gillian laughing.

'I wouldn't dream of it. Saint-Saëns, Schubert . . . Oh, here we are. Under S not P of course. Silly me.' He drew out a distinctive pink and yellow sleeve with black lettering like pieces of torn newsprint. A vulture amongst the pigeons.

'Nothing like a little night music,' said Catherine.

'Have you heard it?' He sounded disappointed. 'It's only just out. Trash Records had almost sold out.' He blew dust off the needle with a sound like a distant explosion. 'Simon says' – Simon was his friend at Cambridge, who was doing research into narrative structures in the novels of Henry Green – 'it reminds him of Rimbaud. Or Lautréamont. I forget which.'

A thunderous drumming made further conversation impossible. The electric whine of guitars was overlaid by a nasal keening. A celebration of vacancy; apposite enough, thought Catherine, amused by Robin's predilection for the theatrical.

Robin himself had the satisfied air of a man displaying his latest first edition. In general, his record collection, like his taste in clothes, was distinctly conservative. In fact, to judge from its pristine ranks of *Deutsche Grammophon* and *Classics for Pleasure*, the popular music of the past twenty years might never have existed. So it was all the more bizarre – although not uncharacteristic of him, Catherine thought – that he should pick up on the youth cult in its terminal stages. Even then, it was as a sort of late flowering of Dadaist or Surrealist art forms rather than as a street fashion that he saw it.

Sounds reminiscent of amplified breaking glass and hammered sheet metal filled the room, in which everyone stood frozen in attitudes of discomfort or feigned indifference. Jonathan flipped idly through a coffee-table sized edition of the works of Marcel Duchamp. Virginia sipped her orange juice. Saul stared grimly out of the window. Gillian looked exasperated.

'Rob, darling, do we *have* to have this?'

Robin's grin faded. 'Sorry.' He lifted the needle from the groove so that the singer was silenced in mid-ejaculation. There was a moment's silence.

'Well,' said Jonathan, 'it certainly makes a change from Vivaldi.'

'I think it's total crap,' said Saul.

'Now, darling, that's not fair,' said Virginia. 'At least it's *different*.'

'In my view,' said Robin pointedly, 'Punk's the most significant thing to have happened since sixty-eight.'

'You have to be kidding.'

'I'm perfectly serious. We're at a watershed. The Sixties is dead, long live the New Wave.'

'It's a kids' fashion,' Saul said contemptuously. 'You remember being a kid, don't you? It's when you do stupid things like taking drugs and sleeping around. Or putting safety-pins through your nose . . .'

'Punk is simply the beginning of the end,' said Robin, with an air of satisfaction. 'The postwar dream is over. Things are falling apart.'

'*Mere anarchy is loosed upon the world*,' murmured Jonathan. 'What *fun*. I must say, I'd be interested to see one of these groups in the flesh.'

'You mean live,' said Saul rudely.

'Live or dead, it doesn't matter. I'd like to see if they look as awful as they sound, that's all.'

'I can get tickets for the End of the World tour at the Playhouse next week, if you really want to go,' Catherine said, amused by the look of incredulity on her lover's face.

'Perhaps we should eat now,' said Gillian, 'or things will start to spoil. I can't think what's happened to Magda . . .'

For the next hour the Orrs' small kitchen was filled with the smell of cooking and the sound of opinionated conversation. Catherine, looking around the table, felt a rush of sentimental affection for her friends which was perhaps not unconnected with the amount of wine she had drunk. At moments like this even the things she disliked about them – their intellectual arrogance, their indifference to anything other than their own concerns – seemed nothing more than endearing foibles. Her gaze flickered briefly over Virginia's face, then back to Saul's. He returned her stare a moment, then looked away. Guilt written all over his face. That was what came of having a highly developed moral sense, she supposed. She herself felt no misgivings about the way things had turned out. Sex without commitment. It was having your cake and eating it.

'The question is,' Robin was saying, 'is it *art*? And if it isn't art, what is it? I mean, no one's denying he can turn a phrase when he wants to and some of his comic insights are extra-ordinary, but . . .'

The discussion around the table was of a writer whose first novel had established him as something of a satirist and whose second had just appeared in paperback.

'Orchestrated misogyny,' said Gillian sourly. 'His women characters are cartoons.'

'I think we've agreed he can't deal with character in the round,' Jonathan murmured, 'but then, in the modern age, who can?'

'I think he writes wonderfully well about sex,' Robin said. 'I laughed out loud at that bit where the dwarf tries to seduce the six-foot Amazon . . . Although I admit his women are caricatures,' he added, glancing at Gillian.

'It's just a lot of sick jokes about sex and death,' she said.

'Should I read this book?' said Saul with sudden interest.

'I suppose you might enjoy it.' Gillian shrugged crossly. 'You're a man.'

'I enjoyed it,' Catherine said. 'I thought it was quite a moral tale.'

'I admire an author who can kill off all his characters on the last page,' said Jonathan. 'It shows a proper disregard for sentimental convention.'

'Whether you like his books or not,' Catherine said, 'you have to admit he's doing something no one else is.'

'Oh absolutely,' Robin said. 'I mean, who wants to read another of those tedious novels where the characters sit around at dinner parties talking about art? That's one area where you Americans have an advantage.' He waved his fork at Saul. 'You've got it all there. The big theme. Right in front of you. Look at Eisenberg, for example. Nothing half-hearted or effete about him. He really gets to grips with the postmodern condition. The decline of Western civilization. The dehumanization of urban life. The death of love.'

'You don't catch him hanging around at dinner parties,' said Saul.

The doorbell went and Robin got up to answer it. When he returned, followed by Magda, it was as if a large and noisy crowd had entered the room. In her billowing kaftan patterned with male and female symbols, she exuded good humour and a fair amount of alcohol. Donald was nowhere to be seen.

'Gillian, I'm *sorry*. Donald insisted we stop off to pick up some wine. That was over an hour ago. I said to him, Donald, we're late. But do you think anything I say or do has any *effect* on that man?'

'Where is Donald, actually?' said Robin. 'Have you left him outside?'

'Oh, he'll be along,' Magda said airily. 'He got talking to someone in the pub. You know Donald, he has no sense of time.'

'We saved you some soup,' Gillian's smile was a little strained. 'I'm afraid it's a bit cold but I can easily . . .'

'Don't bother. Cold is fine.' Magda sat down. 'Well, how goes it? Hi Catherine. Hi Saul. Virginia, you're looking gorgeous. Jonathan, long time no see. How's Walter Pater these days?'

'Oh, you know. Bearing up. I saw Jean Loveless the other day and she quite liked my piece on *Marius the Epicurean*.'

'I heard a story about Jean Loveless.' Magda rolled her eyes lewdly. 'Apparently she's having an affair with someone in the English department . . .'

'Hobson,' suggested Robin with a smirk.

'No, it was a woman.'

'The idea of Hobson having an affair with anyone is just too incredible. Those goloshes. That awful pipe,' said Gillian.

'Francesca Burns,' said Magda. 'Thin, dark, intense. Lectures on Shelley.'

'Francesca? But she's married, surely?'

Magda shrugged. 'It's just a rumour. But the person who told me had good reason to know, because she and Jean had a thing going for years. Then Francesca showed up and *pow*! Love at first sight.'

'More salad, anyone?' said Gillian. 'Magda, this fish has gone a bit dry. I can do you an omelette if you like . . .'

'It looks delicious, really. Anyway, this woman was telling me things had gotten pretty serious. Jean was trying to persuade Francesca to leave her husband and go and live with her and Francesca wouldn't because apparently he had a breakdown last year and she was afraid he might try something stupid . . .'

'What, kill himself you mean?' said Jonathan. 'How *extreme*.'

'I told you, it's only a rumour. For God's sake don't tell anyone I told you . . .'

'What a hotbed of intrigue the English department is these days,' Robin murmured. Behind the steel-rimmed glasses, his eyes gleamed with malicious amusement. 'I wonder what it is about English Literature that encourages adulterous liaisons. More wine, Saul?'

'I'm fine thanks.' Saul's usually sallow face was flushed, Catherine saw. A mixture of alcohol and bad conscience. Under the table she touched his foot with her own and felt him jump as if he had been burned.

'Where would the novel be without adultery?' said Jonathan. 'I mean, look at Flaubert. Tolstoy. Joyce, of course . . .'

'Updike,' said Virginia helpfully.

'Updike, certainly. Bellow. Roth.'

'It's fascinating, this thing about writers and sex,' said Magda, lighting up a mentholated kingsize. 'I mean, Joyce was pretty weird, calling Nora his dark-blue rain-drenched flower and then asking her to shit in her drawers . . .'

'Wonderful word, drawers,' said Jonathan. 'So substantial.'

'There's this terrific letter he wrote Stanislaus from Trieste saying, got to stop now, Nora's trying on a new pair . . .' Magda's laugh ended in a wheezing cough.

'Of course, they were all living together, weren't they?' Robin said. 'Joyce and his brother and Nora.'

'That's right. Stanislaus even supported them for a while.'

'Two men and one woman under one roof,' Robin mused. 'It must have got a bit claustrophobic. Did they have an affair?'

'Nora and Stanislaus? There's no evidence of it,' Magda said thoughtfully. 'Although, of course, you can't rule it out.'

'Certainly not,' said Robin. 'A fruitful subject for postgraduate research there, I'd have thought. Such a resonant theme, infidelity. As a matter of fact, I'm working on a sequence of poems about it.'

'It sounds fascinating,' said Saul.

'Oh it is. Perhaps you'd like to give me your opinion on it, sometime.'

'Anytime,' said Saul.

'I'd love some more dessert.' The sing-song cadences of Virginia's voice dispelled the silence which had appeared, like an uninvited guest, in their midst. 'It's really delicious. What do you put in it? Brandy?'

'Sherry, actually,' said Gillian. 'It's terribly easy. I'll give you the recipe if you like.'

'I guess you have to keep your strength up, right?' said Magda, toying with the whiskery skeleton of her trout. 'It must be great not to have to worry about your figure. How far along are you?'

'About sixteen, no, seventeen weeks.' Virginia glanced at her husband. It was unlike Saul to be so quiet. Maybe he was getting one of his headaches. 'It is seventeen weeks, isn't it, darling?'

'I guess so.'

'Can you feel it moving?' asked Magda.

'Just a little. It's a sort of fluttering. Like heartburn, only different, you know? Sometimes I lie in bed at night and I think I can feel its heart beating. Saul says I'm imagining things.'

'I saw a job in the *TLS* last week,' said Gillian. 'Assistant lecturer at Bradford Poly. No, it was Leeds. Somewhere like that. I thought I might apply . . .'

'Do you still throw up in the mornings?' Magda attacked her trifle with every sign of enjoyment.

'Not any more. It was terrible in the first weeks. I couldn't keep a thing down, could I, Saul?'

'No.' He passed his hand over his eyes. He was getting a migraine, Virginia thought remorsefully. He must have been feeling bad this morning, when he'd said he didn't want to come. And she'd insisted.

'Of course, you never see Oxbridge appointments advertised.' Gillian's voice cracked with indignation. 'Only the boring jobs that nobody wants in out-of-the-way places.'

'We'll go soon,' Virginia murmured in Saul's ear, 'just as soon as we've had some coffee.'

The doorbell rang and kept on ringing, as if someone were leaning on it hard, or had fallen against it.

'That'll be Donald,' Magda sighed. 'Don't get up, Robin. I'll let the bastard in myself.'

'Um, look,' Gillian glanced over her shoulder at the door, as if afraid she might be overheard. 'I'm sorry for what Rob said just now. All that stuff about infidelity. I can't think what got into him.'

A simple desire for revenge, thought Catherine. Or making mischief. 'I don't think anyone noticed.'

'Saul did.' Gillian measured coffee into a paper cone. 'I thought at one point he was going to walk out.'

'He's a little on edge at the moment,' said Catherine. The table in front of her displayed still-life arrangements of consumption and waste: empty bottles, broken crusts.

'I'm not surprised.' Gillian scraped remnants of food and cigarette ends into the bin. 'She seems quite pleasant,' she said, after a pause. 'Not quite what I expected.'

'Oh, she is,' said Catherine. 'Very pleasant.'

'Almost too pleasant, in a way. I suppose Americans are like that.'

'Yes.'

There was a subdued roar and a fragrant cloud of steam as the coffee finished percolating. Gillian set out cups and saucers for eight. 'What do you think you'll do?' she said.

'There's nothing much I can do.'

'You could move out, I suppose. Rob and I could put you up here for a bit.'

'Thanks. But I don't want to move. Liz needs the money. And besides, it would only draw attention to the situation.'

'Doesn't she know? I'd assumed that was why she came. To rescue him from your clutches.'

'She doesn't know.'

'Well she soon will if things go on like this.' Gillian began to laugh softly, her shoulders shaking. 'I'm sorry. It's just that it was so funny, what Rob was saying . . . about two women and one man . . . no, the other way around . . . I thought I'd burst out laughing.'

'I suppose it does have its farcical side,' said Catherine.

In the Orrs' sitting room Donald was sprawled on the sofa, a glass of wine in his hand. His face was flushed, his voice loud.

'Of course Spenser was a complete fascist,' he said. 'Look at his views on Ireland.'

'That's a pretty simplistic attitude.' Saul's smile was that of a man about to lose his temper. He'd had just about enough. First that bastard Robin, playing his stupid games. Now this arrogant jerk.

'Not at all. It's all there, in black and white. The Irish are seen as racially inferior. Sub-human.'

'If you're referring to *A View of the State of Ireland*, I think you'll find that interpretation was discredited some time ago,' Saul said coldly.

'I was talking about *The Faerie Queene*. The whole thing's a denunciation of the Other. The Outsider, the Catholic, the Jew . . .'

'I totally disagree. It's a poem about love. About embracing the Other, if you like.' Saul permitted himself a smile. The guy called himself a writer. A lot he knew about it. Trying to impose his crass political interpretations on great art.

'Oh, there's sex in it of course. If you like that kind of thing. A touch precious for my taste.' Donald hooked his long legs over the end of the sofa and settled the cushions more firmly under his head; the attitude of a man so certain of winning his argument that he finds the effort of doing so fatiguing. He yawned hugely. 'But the prevailing impression I take away from it is one of hatred. Hatred for sex, hatred for women . . .'

'No – '

'Hatred for anything that's not your bloody Protestant Aryan true-blue Brit.'

'You're wrong. You're so wrong.'

'I have to admit,' said Virginia placidly, 'it's refreshing to find someone who doesn't like Spenser. Sometimes I think I'll go crazy if I have to hear another word about him. Spenser this, Spenser that . . .'

'It's his ideas I can't stomach.' Donald belched softly. 'His poetry's alright. Some of it's very fine.'

'Well that's a relief.' There was an edge of sarcasm to Saul's voice. 'For a minute you had me worried I was wasting my time.'

'You are.' Donald scratched his armpit thoughtfully. 'The whole thing's a bloody waste of time. Research!' He spat the word out as if it had a bad taste. 'What use is any of it to anyone?'

'Oh God . . .' Magda covered her face with her hands.

'Oh, come on,' said Robin mildly, 'I don't agree with that. It's a job like any other, surely?'

'Parasites.' Donald shook his head slowly from side to side. 'You're nothing but a bunch of parasites. Never done a day's real work in your lives.'

Saul left the room.

'How is it different from, ah, being a writer, for example?' said Gillian.

'There's a world of difference,' Donald said solemnly. 'A world of difference.' He reached over and switched on the Orrs' portable television set. The rubbery features of the President of the United States, answering questions at a White House press conference, appeared on the screen, followed by an archive clip of the Six Day War. Tanks moving across desert terrain. Barbed wire. A burst of sniper fire. 'Look at that,' Donald said. 'That's the real world. What do any of you know about the real world?'

'Oh, for fuck's sake,' said Magda, 'we can't all be toting Kalashnikovs.'

'I think you'd look awfully fetching in uniform,' said Jonathan. 'Olive-green fatigues and one of those nifty little forage caps.'

'Someone has to guard the flame of culture I suppose . . .' Donald gave a derisive snicker.

'Well, goodness,' Gillian sounded indignant, 'what's wrong with that? I should have thought you, of all people . . .'

'Oh, Donald doesn't include himself in the parasite class,'

said Magda. 'It's only us academics he wants to send to the salt-mines.'

'*Not that one!*'

Catherine, about to extinguish her cigarette in a bakelite ashtray shaped like the ace of clubs, was prevented from doing so by Robin's shout of alarm.

'We don't actually *use* that,' he murmured apologetically. 'It's terribly fragile. Early thirties, you know. Very collectable. Try the kitchen. There should be a saucer you can use.'

In the narrow passage she encountered Saul, coming out of the bathroom. Without a word he pushed her against the wall and began to kiss her, thrusting his tongue deep in her mouth. His knee nudged her legs apart. For a soundless, undignified moment they grappled together behind the door. Then she pulled away, her lips smarting pleasantly.

'Idiot,' she said.

In the kitchen she took her time sorting through the pieces of unwashed crockery until she found what she was looking for. She knocked the feathery tip of ash off the end of her cigarette and replaced it between her lips, drawing deeply on the cool tainted smoke. Shaking a little, she ran cold water over each wrist in turn, the blue vein jumping like a snake beneath the skin. Her reflection in the dark windowpane observed these actions. It smiled, her *doppelgänger*, sensing the discomfiture of its corporeal twin.

8

'Cathy's a strange girl, isn't she?'

'Is she?' Saul did not look up from the book he was reading. Beside him, on the bed, Virginia yawned and stretched. Late-afternoon sun filled the room, glancing off polished surfaces.

'You know what I mean. She told me the other day about all these relationships she's had. With all kinds of guys. As if it wasn't important, you know. Just something that happened.'

'Maybe it was.'

'It's kind of immature, don't you think?'

'Yes.'

'Do you find her attractive?'

'Who, Catherine? She's not my type.'

'You have to admit she's attractive. I mean, if you ignore the way she dresses . . .'

'She's neurotic.'

'She has a nice figure. And her hair is nice.'

'What *is* this? Virginia, I'm trying to do some work here . . .'

'I was just trying to figure out why she doesn't have a boyfriend.'

'I already told you, she's crazy. Weird.'

'Some men like that kind of woman.'

'That's their problem.' He stroked the damp hair back from her forehead. 'Now will you let me finish this? I've got a paper to write. And you're supposed to be resting.'

'Sorry.' She folded her hands over the hard dome of her belly and lay for a while, watching the dancing reflections on the ceiling. 'Saul?'

'What is it?' His voice betrayed a certain tension, which

was perhaps no more than impatience at being interrupted. He closed the book with a snap.

'You're not unhappy about anything, are you? I mean . . . the baby.'

'Don't be silly.' Perhaps out of remorse for having spoken sharply, or relief that she had not asked a different question, he leaned over and kissed her on the lips.

'It's just that sometimes you seem so . . . well, *distant*. As if you were thinking about something else all the time . . .'

'I'm sorry.' He closed his eyes. 'I've been so busy,' he said.

'I know. I'm not complaining. I just want things to be all right between us . . .'

'Everything's just fine.' He put his arm around her, cradling her against his chest, a tender yet slightly awkward position, in which she could no longer see his face. 'Say, why don't we eat out tonight? We could go to a movie if you like.'

'Sounds good.' Not for the first time, she had the feeling he was being evasive. Ever since she had told him about the baby, he'd been acting strangely. As if he had something on his mind. His behaviour was inconsistent. Some days, he would be cold and distant towards her; at other times, he was consideration itself. Perhaps it was jealousy. Fear of losing her attention. It happened sometimes, she knew. Maybe she should ask him . . . yet something held her back.

'Let's do it,' he said, dropping a kiss on the top of her head. 'And now I really have to finish this chapter.'

Funny how there was always a chapter to finish, Virginia thought.

In the Botanical Gardens the rhododendrons were in flower, their petals the colour of lipstick. Hard green leaves made a screen against the sun for the lovers underneath. Greenish leaf-shadows on pale faces sweaty with too much kissing. The earth beneath the glossy, spear-pointed leaves, the purplish clusters of blossom, had a rank smell of urine and leaf mould. In the hot noon sun it was the only cool spot, dark with its own darkness, like a shuttered room on a hot day. Their faces were in shadow, broken into dancing white shapes by the moving screen above their heads. When they stood up, stiff and a little chilled in spite of the heat of the day, there was a pattern of criss-crossed leaves and broken stalks incised on the palms of their hands.

'Don't ask me what we're going to do. I don't know what we're going to do. Do you know what we're going to do?'

'No.'

'Let's walk.'

They rose and began to follow the circular path that would lead them, by way of the arboretum, the rock garden and the azalea lawn, back to their point of departure.

'Are you suggesting we tell her? Is that it?'

'Of course not.'

They entered the little wilderness. Sunlight filtered through transparent leaves of beech and oak. An aeroplane drew its vapour trail across the sky, like a pencil across a page.

'What's she doing today?' Somehow, they always ended up talking about Virginia. Hers was the spectral presence at their meetings, the silent witness of their clandestine couplings.

'Shopping. She's always shopping. Things for the baby. Clothes. None of her things fit her anymore.'

'Poor Virginia.'

He looked at her sharply. 'You don't have to feel sorry for her.'

'Why shouldn't I feel sorry for her? I like her.'

'Okay, okay . . .'

'Believe me, I wish I didn't. It would make things a lot easier.'

Loitering in the knot garden, where clipped box hedges formed a pattern of entwined scrolls, hearts and lozenges, they held hands and kissed, like sulky adolescents delaying the moment of parting at the school gates.

'I have to get back. She's expecting me.'

'I'm going back to the library.' Catherine took his arm. A

gust of wind blew petals of white blossom onto their hair. 'Look,' she said. 'Snow. Remember that week it snowed so hard and we spent most of the time in bed?'

'You know I do. Can I see you tomorrow night?'

'I can't make it tomorrow.' She looked at him slyly. 'Jonathan and I are going to watch the end of the world at the Playhouse.'

'That guy. I don't know what you see in him.'

'I like him.'

'So it seems. Are you sleeping with him?'

'As a matter of fact I'm not. He prefers boys, unfortunately.'

'You must have a lot in common.'

They walked for a while in silence, until they reached the intersection where they were to separate.

'Look,' said Saul, 'I'm sorry for what I said just now . . .'

'Forget it.' Out of the corner of her eye, she saw the Queen of Spades lying face up in the gutter.

'No, I mean it. Really. I just feel so confused about the whole thing . . .'

'It doesn't matter.' She turned to go, but he put out a hand to detain her.

'I guess I'm in love with you,' he said unhappily.

If Catherine's relationship with Saul had lapsed into a somewhat desultory affair, her relationship with Virginia seemed, incongruously, to be growing more intense. The more time she spent with the other woman, the harder it was to resist the subtle inducements of her charm. Everything about Virginia fascinated her: the way she looked, the things she said. She wondered, for a time, if what she felt was sexual attraction, but decided the explanation was more complex than that; it seemed connected to the desire she felt, always, to control situations. There was a perverse pleasure in being at once the friend and the betrayer, Catherine found. It was within her power to effect a good deal of damage, by the simple expedient of telling Virginia everything. Yet she chose to say nothing. Virginia was her friend. She had no wish to hurt her. But there was a piquancy in the knowledge that she could, if she wanted to.

'What are you wearing tonight?'

'I don't know. Jeans, I suppose. My black T-shirt.'

'That ripped old thing? It's kind of tacky, isn't it?'

'That's the idea.'

They were in the kitchen, drinking tea. The table was piled high with plastic carrier bags containing the purchases Virginia had made that afternoon. Nursing brassieres. Voluminous nightdresses. Skirts with expandable waistlines.

'Hideous, aren't they?' Virginia said.

'Not very alluring.'

'They make them like that on purpose.' Virginia cut herself a slice of cake and licked the crumbs from her fingers. 'To stop us feeling sexy. Pregnant women aren't supposed to feel sexy.'

'Does it work?' Catherine said lightly. Pregnancy had given Virginia an almost supernatural look, she thought. The rich blood pulsing through her veins heightened the colour in her cheeks. The whites of her eyes were bluish with health.

'Not at all,' Virginia said. 'Which is maybe just as well, with a husband like mine. Sometimes I get the feeling all that man thinks about is sex.'

'Don't they all?'

'I couldn't really say. Saul was my first, you know. I mean, I had friends in high school who were sleeping with their boyfriends at thirteen but I was always kind of old fashioned. I never wanted that kind of relationship, until I met Saul. I guess that sounds pretty boring . . .'

'Not half as boring as having sex with a lot of people you don't like.'

'Poor Cathy. What you need is a nice, normal guy, instead of all these creeps and weirdos you keep ending up with.'

'I don't think I know any nice, normal guys, unfortunately.'

'Oh, come on. You just haven't tried. You know, you could be very attractive if you worked at it a little more . . .'

'Do you think so?' It was hard to tell how much calculation there was behind Virginia's remarks, Catherine thought. Perhaps it was this she found so disarming.

'Sure I do. I'm talking about your clothes mainly. And your hair.' Absent-mindedly, she began to play with Catherine's hair, lifting a piece of the pale flat stuff and rubbing it between her fingers as if it were poor quality cloth. 'You have nice hair,' she murmured. 'Really. You should do something with it. Maybe cut it. Have you thought about getting it cut?'

'Once or twice.' Catherine sat, transfixed by the other woman's touch. She found she was holding her breath. She had an image of herself reaching over and taking Virginia's face between her hands, slowly kissing her mouth. The thought raised interesting possibilities. Then the front door slammed.

'Hi honey,' Virginia said, as Saul came in, dropping his coat and briefcase on the chair. 'Did you want some tea?'

'I'd love some tea.' He kissed his wife, then looked at Catherine. 'Saw that friend of yours. Said he'd pick you up at seven.' She was blushing, he noticed. Maybe she had something going with this guy after all.

'Thanks,' she said, recovering her composure in a second. 'I suppose I'd better put on my glad rags.'

'I still think you should wear something different,' said Virginia. 'I mean, what's the poor guy going to think if you show up for a first date wearing jeans and a ripped shirt? Men like a woman to take a little trouble with her appearance, don't they, darling?'

'Things are different over here,' said Saul. 'Is there anything to eat? I missed lunch today.'

'Have some cake,' said Catherine, pushing the plate towards him.

*

'Have we time for a drink?' Jonathan's expression, as he regarded the crowd of garishly painted adolescents amongst which they found themselves, was one of comical dismay. 'I see there's no licence.'

'Most of the clientele are underage. Or they prefer other stimulants.'

'They do seem disgustingly young.' His voice was loud enough to attract stares from the group nearest to them, whey-faced fifteen-year-olds in carefully torn clothes, the effect augmented with a decorative flourish or two: safety-pins inserted through cheek or earlobe, toilet-chain necklaces. 'And disappointingly ugly. They must have had to work hard to achieve that degree of grub-like pallor. Years of eating chips or whatever they eat, one imagines . . .'

'There's a pub across the road,' said Catherine. The stares were becoming increasingly hostile. She was starting to regret the impulse which had led her to propose the outing. Jonathan, however, seemed to be enjoying himself.

In the pub he gave his order in ringing tones. 'Give me a whisky. Make that two. No, not that rubbish. The malt.'

The pub was a draughty, sparsely furnished barn. Conversation was difficult against a background noise of confused shouting from the darts players in the back room and the football commentary from the TV over the bar. The air was thick with smoke and the carpet with its pattern of swirling leaves was pitted with burns.

'So tell me,' Jonathan said, 'do you do this sort of thing often?'

'It depends what you mean.'

He smiled. 'Believe it or not,' he said, 'I used to frequent these sort of places once. Not here, of course, but at home. There was one pub in particular I used to go to. On the seafront. I don't suppose you know Brighton do you?'

'A bit.'

'Terrible place. The pub, not the town. Full of junkies and pushers. Prostitutes. Dreadful old men. I used to think the

people one met in places like that were more, you know, *real*.'
Jonathan frowned at his drink, turning the chipped glass round. 'Whereas in fact they're just as unreal as everyone else. Probably more so.'

'I think the main attraction of places like these is their anonymity,' said Catherine, considering, as she spoke, the wisdom of making a confidant of Jonathan. But then it occurred to her that she didn't much care who got to hear of her indiscretions. 'I mean, for example, if you wanted to pick somebody up, this is the perfect place.'

'I take it you speak from experience?'

'Yes. Fairly recent experience, as a matter of fact. I thought it might cure me of wanting to sleep with other people's husbands.'

'And did it?'

'No.'

'How *is* Saul? Such a brusque young man. He was distinctly hostile at our last meeting.'

'He's hostile to everyone at the moment. I don't think the prospect of fatherhood agrees with him.'

A hoarse shout from the group of players in the back room greeted the placing of an arrow smack in the centre of the board.

'I suppose it must feel uncomfortably like being a grown up. Poor chap. Does his wife know, do you think?'

'What, about how he feels, or . . .'

'No, *no*. I mean about you, of course. About this thing you've got going with her husband.'

'No.'

'I quite liked her, you know,' said Jonathan. 'Thought she seemed rather sweet.'

'She is sweet,' Catherine said, with more sharpness than she'd intended. 'Everyone likes her. *I* like her, if it comes to that . . .'

'Perhaps you'll end up falling in love with both of them,' he said. 'A real *ménage à trois*.'

'I'm not in love with Saul.'

'Of course you're not.' Jonathan finished his drink. 'Only don't say I didn't warn you. Married men are nothing but trouble.'

'I'll bear it in mind,' she said.

'Speaking of brusque young men,' Jonathan said, 'I think it's time I had another chat with the barman. Same again, or would you prefer something more in keeping with these louche surroundings?'

'Let me get them.'

'I wouldn't hear of it. It's the least I can do in return for the evening's entertainment.'

'I'll have a whisky.'

'Sensible girl. And then you can tell me all about your adventures in the skin trade.'

Alone at the table in the centre of the big, half-empty room, its flimsy raft of tables and bentwood chairs adrift upon a sea of smoke, Catherine speculated on the way the evening might have developed had she been unaccompanied – some squalid episode in the back seat of a wrecked cinema with a pallid, sweaty youth whose name she would have had trouble recalling next day – and was glad, on the whole, of Jonathan's presence. Maybe sordid sex had lost its charms for her at last.

Abandon hope all you who enter here,' said Jonathan as they went in, past thickset bouncers in pink frilled shirts and velvet suits, to the hall where a strangely subdued crowd sat in orderly rows, like children on a school outing. As infernos go, it was something of a disappointment. A handful of youths bobbed jerkily up and down below the stage, to the accompaniment of the cracked anthems issuing from loud-speakers, but this was the only sign of the disorder to come.

> Anarchy in the UK
> Is coming someday
> Maybe . . .

So far it seemed a decorous kind of anarchy. Gangs of skinny boys in studded dog collars and school blazers a size too small roamed the aisles, looking for action. Very young girls in black lipstick and heavy black eyeliner fine-tuned their backcombing.

'Bergen-Belsen,' murmured Jonathan, indicating a pubescent girl with a shaven head a few rows in front of them. 'Or Hieronymous Bosch.'

Suddenly the house lights went out. There was a desultory cheer. Whistling. Ironic clapping.

'Just like Covent Garden,' said Jonathan.

A trio of sluttish girls in leopardskin and leather shuffled onstage, carrying electric guitars. They were greeted with hoots of derision and a hail of flying sputum. An earsplitting whine of feedback filled the auditorium, drowning the hoarse shouts of the crowd together with those of the singer, a tawdry harpy with snaky locks, whose mouth seemed to open and close without sound.

'The audience doesn't seem very appreciative,' said Jonathan, bemused. 'Some of them are spitting.'

'Those are the ones that enjoyed it.'

The girls were replaced by a sarcastic Mancunian. His humorous contempt for his audience was clearly reciprocated. After a short harangue on a number of vaguely political themes, he launched into the first of several songs, delivered at great speed and with exaggerated scorn.

'That one shows promise,' Jonathan said. 'Pity about the acne.'

A few minutes elapsed between the second act and the final one. Overweight men in T-shirts and flared jeans, which slipped down to expose the crack between their buttocks as they stooped, moved equipment about the stage.

'If this is the future, it seems a rather depressing one,' said Jonathan. 'Ugly clothes, bad skin and premature deafness.'

The lights went out. From the darkness twin searchlights raked the audience, sirens wailed. The trappings of fascism were in vogue that year. When the safety curtain rose four black-uniformed figures stood silhouetted against the backdrop of a British flag, massively enlarged. There was silence. The four held their bad boy pose – legs apart, instruments cocked – for a couple of seconds, then stepped forward. Blood-red flares lit the stage as they struck the first chord, a choppy, broken sound resembling nothing so much as old-fashioned machine-gun fire. A sound from the movies, Catherine thought.

Jonathan said something close to her ear, she couldn't hear what. Everything was lost in a deafening surge of noise. White noise. Noise without form, without meaning. The crowd was on its feet. A trembling, ecstatic crew. Dancers slammed their bodies into the front of the stage like flagellants in a mediaeval Dance of Death. Sweat and saliva made a rainbow haze in the white light.

At the point at which it seemed as if the sound must go on for ever, until the walls around them disintegrated and time ran backwards, the music stopped and the writhing dancers subsided. Catherine looked at her companion. He was shaking his head, as if to dislodge water in the ears. She looked around at the sweating faces, the glazed eyes of those around her and felt a sudden revulsion. There was a boy standing next to her in a Union Jack T-shirt emblazoned with swastikas, *Love* tattooed on one hand, *Hate* on the other. On her other side, a girl with burned-out eyes, black lipsticked lips, swayed in a trance of pleasure. Typist by day, maenad by night. Catherine shivered, seeing perhaps an image of her own split self. Her ears hurt, she wanted to weep. She could not tell whether this was an emanation of her psychic state or merely the contagious hysteria of the crowd. What, after all, did any of them want? To lose themselves for an hour in the general pulse, the rhythms of pleasure. Surrender was so easy. All it required was to let go.

As for herself, what was she doing there? Her presence was false, an act of intellectual tourism. Jonathan was right. The whole thing was unreal. Nothing but a consumer fantasy for kids, offering safe violence, safe death. A temporary annihilation.

The lead singer came to the front of the stage. He was dressed, as were the others, in a one-piece garment, zipped and flapped with extraneous pockets, tags, epaulets and thongs, suggesting some industrial or fetishistic purpose.

'The next one,' he said with polite venom, 'is about Armageddon.'

'I suppose one might have guessed,' said Jonathan.

When it was over, they wandered out into the silent streets, their ears ringing with pressure.

'Well,' said Jonathan cordially, 'a most interesting experience. Not one I should care to repeat, but still . . .'

'I'm glad you enjoyed it.'

'I wouldn't have missed it for the world. That sinister boy with the bad teeth. That atrocious music. So violent. So *inhuman*. I'm sure it must mean something. The end of civilization perhaps.' He yawned. 'But then again, perhaps not. Gód, I'm exhausted.'

'It's the noise. And the heat.'

'I'll see you home. No, really, I insist. A delightful evening. I don't know how I can reciprocate. I've got tickets for *Lohengrin* next week, but it hardly seems like a fair exchange . . .'

'There is one thing you can do for me,' Catherine said.

9

Virginia contemplated the Madonna. The Madonna's pose was severe, the folds of her scarlet dress and light blue robe stiffly pleated, so that is was hard to discern the living body underneath. Her long slender hands were placed together, the fingertips touching, in pious invocation. Her gaze was lowered so that only a narrow gleam of eyeball was visible. On the ground where she knelt in prayer lay the figure of a naked child. In the background, behind the Madonna's veiled head, were broken columns, the ruins of a Roman temple.

Virginia looked at the Madonna's sweet, submissive mouth, her folded hands, for a long time. Something about the image was disturbing, she could not decide what. She looked at the smooth forehead beneath the transparent wisp of veil and at the place where the Madonna's breasts should have been, beneath the close-fitting bodice. Her own breasts felt lumpy and distended. As she had dressed that morning she had observed with fascination the branching blue veins which ran towards the aureolae, visible beneath the skin. What was happening to her? Her body no longer seemed her own.

Virginia's feet were hurting, her small ankles felt swollen with fluid. She looked again at the kneeling woman and then at the child. The precocious awareness of His gaze was disconcerting, made Him seem, somehow, more adult than His girlish mother. Virginia felt a sudden stirring, like a premonition of disaster. Pressing her hands to her heart in unconscious imitation of the Virgin, she sat down on the three-cornered love-seat in the centre of the gallery. As she waited for the spasm to pass, envisaging the movement of some blind, deep-sea creature, her mind returned to the quarrel she'd had the previous night with Saul.

*

'So what do you think?'

'What do I think about what?' They were in bed. Saul was reading. As he turned a page, ash fell from his half-smoked cigarette onto the sheets. 'Shit,' he said, brushing it away. Virginia flinched. She hated him smoking, especially in bed.

'I asked you what you thought about staying here until the baby comes. Or if we should try and go home. If we decide to go, it has to be soon, because I won't be able to travel . . .'

'So stay.' He did not raise his eyes from the page.

'Don't you think we should discuss it a little?'

'What's to discuss? You want to stay, we'll stay. You want to go, we'll go. It's your decision.'

'I want to know what you think.' His casualness infuriated her. She felt the swollen sensation at the back of her throat that was the prelude to weeping.

'And I've just told you. Isn't that good enough?'

'No.' Her voice cracked with the strain of holding back tears. She heard him sigh with exasperation. He closed the book, folding the piece of paper he had been using to mark the place inside it, on which a few words were written in an unfamiliar hand. The bedsprings jangled as he turned to face her. The mattress was an old one which sagged in the middle, so that both partners gravitated towards the centre of the bed during the night. In the mornings Virginia woke with her face pressed against Saul's back, or half-smothered by the weight of his outflung arm.

'What's the matter?' he said. 'You seem a little upset.'

'I'm not upset. I just asked you a simple question. All I want is a simple answer . . .'

'I did give you an answer.'

'But you don't seem to think it's important enough to think about even for a second.'

'I do think it's important.'

'Maybe it doesn't matter to you where your child is born.'

'I didn't say that. What I said was *you* make the decision. It's your baby.'

'I don't believe I'm hearing this . . .' She began to cry. Her voice had an ugly sound, a note of shrill complaint. 'You talk as if it's nothing to do with you. *I* should make the decision. It's not your responsibility, right?'

'Baby . . .' He put his arms around her, but she pulled away.

'Don't call me that.' She wiped her eyes with the back of her hand. Her chest ached with an unpleasant sensation of fullness, as if from a poorly digested meal. 'Just leave me alone.'

Saul looked at her for a minute, then shrugged. He opened the book he had been reading and the slip of paper fell out. He picked it up and began to wind it around his fingers.

It was cool in the gallery. Its walls of green watered silk, its diffuse lighting, had a soothing effect on Virginia's nerves. Outside the streets were filled with the harsh glare of noon. Shadows were annihilated, colours bled of their substance. Here it was all muted half-tones, subtle gradations. Flesh into earth, earth into stone. Fingertips barely touching. She looked from the Madonna to the child and back again. The Madonna's face was pale green, the result of centuries of devout obeisance – the touch of lips, of hands wearing away the pigment to reveal the under-painting.

She looked at her watch and saw her appointment at the hospital was not for another twenty minutes. She had time to phone Saul. She'd left him working at home that morning, while she went shopping. There'd been a coolness between them, because of last night. She knew she'd been unfair, expecting him to make a decision about the baby when he had such a lot of other things on his mind. She would tell him she was sorry for the things she'd said.

If there were difficulties, only half perceived, but nonetheless felt, in being the injured party in the affair, these were nothing compared to the agonies of mind experienced by the guilty. If the expression of that agony was stifled by the need for concealment, that only made it more acute. At least, that was Saul's experience. Confronted on all sides by evidence of his fatal prevarication, he felt himself paralysed, like a man contemplating suicide who hesitates between alternative modes of self-destruction – death by water, poison, defenestration or the noose.

There were times when he saw himself as culpable, others when he seemed to himself to be curiously blameless. It was not he who had instigated the affair with Catherine, just as it had not been his decision to conceive the child his wife was carrying. In this, as in other things, he saw his role as that of a mere functionary. He was, he sometimes felt, little more than a lay figure, arranged into a variety of poses by a controlling hand.

Alone in the apartment, he waited for Catherine. Virginia would not be back from the hospital till four. His gaze wandered idly over the papers spread out in front of him on the table, as if the answer to the conundrum of his relationship with his lover might lie there, amongst the typewritten lines criss-crossed with corrections and erasures and ringed with stains from coffee cups. His fingers gently tapped the edges of the worn volume open on his desk, the coarse yellowing pages crumbling at the margin, dog-eared and soiled with use.

> Then do no further goe, no further stray,
> But here lie downe, and to thy reste betake,
> Th'ill to prevent, that life ensewen may.
> For what hath life, that may it loved make,
> And gives not rather cause it to forsake?
> Feare, sicknesse, age . . .

We cancel each other out, he thought; we're too much alike. An image of her face with its sulky red mouth, its watchful eyes, rose in his mind. He scribbled a note, *cf*

Hamlet: a consummation devoutly to be wished, at the top of a typed sheet.

> Feare, sicknesse, age, losse, labour, sorrow, strife,
> Paine, hunger, cold, that makes the heart to quake;
> And ever fickle fortune rageth rife . . .

But the trials of the Red Cross Knight in the Cave of Suicide failed to engage his attention. What was keeping her for Christ's sake? It was past one. In the dressing-table mirror his face was a wan ghost. He lit a cigarette and stared at his notes. The typed lines danced in and out of focus.

> And ever fickle fortune rageth rife . . .

He had written nothing all morning. He had nothing to say. His mind was vacant, a bubble of spun glass.

The summer had been intolerable. He was racked by guilt and desire in varying intensities. There were times when thoughts of his lover brought him close to rage. Disgust filled him for her petulant moods, her solipsism. In such a mood he would rush to confront her, to end it once and for all. And yet it was not so easy to give her up. People are sicknesses for each other, she had once said, laughing as if she guessed the ambivalence of his feelings towards her.

What made the situation worse, he thought, was that it was he who had caused it, by his own cowardice. If only he had been honest with Virginia when he'd had the chance. Instead, he found himself wandering deeper into a labyrinth of lies. The thought of his wife made him flinch with a peculiarly painful mixture of emotions, of which shame was the strongest. He knew he was behaving in an unpardonable way. He had betrayed her, there was no escaping the fact. But what was he to do? He felt himself the victim of circumstance.

Images of his two women, the dark and the fair, alternated in his mind's eye like the flashing of a strobe. Virginia as he had seen her that morning getting dressed. Her clumsy body with its taut belly held in front of her like a parcel she was afraid to drop. The skin of her abdomen shiny and hard as an onion, striped with a vertical band of darker pigment from navel to pubis. Her blue-veined, swollen breasts. Seeing her like this, it was hard to recall the girl he'd married. God, she was beautiful, then. Black hair, blue eyes. So slender and fine-boned he'd worried about hurting her the first time they'd made love. *Lady, shall I lie in your lap?* He'd been crazy for her that first summer.

His wife's dark-haired image, her faintly tremulous expression, was overlaid by another. Catherine's eyes half-closed at the point of orgasm, a sliver of gleaming white visible beneath the lids. *The lineaments of gratified desire.* He dozed, his head on his hands, in the sweltering heat. A trapped fly crashed against the windowpane. Disease was the wrong analogy, he thought. Love was more like a drug. There was the same kind of instant ecstasy, of temporary release. He'd taken LSD a few times as a student. He remembered the metallic taste it left in the mouth, the momentary vertigo as it took effect. A mixture of pleasant and unpleasant sensations. Not unlike falling in love.

He got up to let the fly out of the room. The sun blazed down on the white street, a dry well between shuttered houses. The shirt he had put on that morning was stained in dark circles under the arms. In the bathroom he stripped to the waist, watching himself in the mirror as he diligently soaped his armpits. Beneath the brown, close-textured skin the musculature was hard and well-defined. He preened a little. A handsome devil. Running water hid the click of the front door, so that he jumped when Catherine's arms encircled his waist from behind.

'You took your time.'

'I had things to do.' She averted her cheek from his kiss, yawning, and began to unbutton her blouse. He followed her into her room, the painted bower. The other room had too many tangible reminders of Virginia; everything – her make-up on the dressing-table, a discarded blouse on the back of a chair, the white lace shawl she'd spread across the bed – reproached him for his importunate desires.

Catherine peeled off her jeans, wriggling her hips, a lewd Calypso. When she was naked she turned to face him. 'Come on,' she said with an ironic look, 'we don't have much time. I'm meeting Jonathan at three.'

'That fairy.'

'He's going to give me a spare key so we can use his room.'

He stared at her, outraged. 'You told him about us?'

'Why not? It's not exactly a secret. Anyway, he said he doesn't mind a bit. As long as we change the sheets.'

'I don't care if he minds or he doesn't mind. *I* mind. You're suggesting we use his room, his bed . . .'

'He won't be sharing it with us, as far as I know.' She looked at her watch. 'An hour,' she said briskly. 'Then I have to go.'

It was with a sense of ill-usage, of having been in some way betrayed, that he took her in his arms. *Discussing me with that guy.* Anger gave an edge to his desire. Not for the first time he felt he wanted to hurt her. But she, with maddening perversity, took his insults for endearments, his injuries for caresses. He thrust into her. When he came, it felt like getting even.

They were getting dressed when the phone rang. Catherine answered it. 'Oh, hello,' she said. 'Yes, he's here.' She handed the phone to Saul, raising her eyebrows. 'Virginia,' she mouthed.

He felt the blood rush to his face. 'Hi, darling. Anything wrong?' It was an effort to control his voice. 'Oh good. It's just you don't usually . . .' He had the sensation his heart was beating too fast. 'Sure . . . I understand . . . Honey, you don't have to apologize . . . I said some things I didn't mean, too . . . Of course I care. You know I do. I love you too, angel,' he murmured, looking at Catherine, leaning, half-clothed, in the doorway.

The grossly inflated abdomen of the woman sitting next to Virginia in the hospital waiting room looked as if it might contain something larger than a human being. A young horse, perhaps. Measuring the other's bulk against her own, more modest size, she pictured long limbs folded under, a nodding, equine head.

'Your first, is it?' Her furtive look had been intercepted.

'That's right.'

Sharp bright eyes flicked over Virginia's face, down to her belly and back again. The red-haired woman smiled. 'Och, the first one's always the worst. I had a terrible time with mine.' The way she said it, the word had a drawn out, guttural quality. *Terr-rrible*. 'When are you due?' Her face was a mass of freckles, Virginia saw. Constellations of tiny brown pinpricks, increasing in density around the eyes and across the bridge of the nose, so that the effect was of a freckled mask.

'October. You?'

'Mine's supposed to be October as well. But they'll no' let it run to term. No' with twins.'

'You're lucky to be having twins.'

'I wouldn't call it lucky. Look at it this way. There's two of them in there,' she slapped her hard round stomach familiarly, 'so there's twice as many things to go wrong. Either they strangle each other on the cord or they suffocate each other on the way out.'

'It sounds like war.'

'That's what it is. Nothing but bloody murder from start to finish. Sleep's impossible. The minute one stops kicking, the other wakes up and starts plunging around.' Leaning over with difficulty, she reached into the bag on the floor between her widespread knees and took out a packet of cigarettes. Bony freckled fingers ripped the cellophane. Watching her,

142

Virginia wondered if the rest of her was as stippled with darker pigment as the visible part. Freckles on her chest, belly and back. Between her toes and in the hollows of elbows and knees. 'Smoke?' she said.

'No, thanks.'

The red-haired woman lit a cigarette and inhaled deeply with a little grunt of pleasure. Under her thin smock, stretched tight across the mountainous bulge, a seismic tremor could be seen.

'Look at that.' She slapped her hand down viciously. 'It's awake. Wee *bastard*.'

'It must be bad at night,' Virginia said.

'Oh, God. Terrible.' The woman exhaled smoke in twin plumes from her nostrils. 'I'll tell you something – after this I'm getting my tubes tied. I told my husband, I said, I'm no' going through this again for you nor anyone.'

'Mrs Meyer.'

'It was nice meeting you,' said Virginia.

Princes Street was awash with red, white and blue bunting. To the displays of spinning wheels and tartans in souvenir shop windows had been added the image of a blandly smiling crowned head. Even the groups of loitering punks at the intersection of Hanover and Rose Street had entered into the spirit of the thing, with faces painted in the ubiquitous colours and the monarch's face, gagged and blindfolded, displayed on their chests.

Walking home, Virginia ran into Liz, a sunburnt dairymaid in a sleevelesss linen smock and a straw hat. She took Virginia's arm.

'Are you heading back? I'll walk with you.' She relieved Virginia of her shopping bag. 'Give me that. You shouldn't be dragging heavy weights about in this heat.'

'I don't have a lot of choice, these days,' said Virginia.

Liz smiled thinly. There was an awkwardness about her behaviour towards the American girl which was missing from her dealings with the rest of the household. More than once Virginia had detected a certain reserve in Liz's manner, as if, in some way, she made the other woman uncomfortable. Saul had told her Liz was having problems conceiving. Poor thing, it must be hard for her with a pregnant woman in the house, Virginia thought.

'I suppose not. You look done in though. Are you feeling alright?'

'I'll be fine.' Virginia managed a smile, although the examination had left her feeling bruised all over. Mr Forster had had his team of students with him that afternoon and encouraged each of them in turn to probe her reluctant flesh. 'I guess it's the effect my gynaecologist has on me . . .'

'Is he nice?'

'Gorgeous. Saul's terribly jealous.'

Liz laughed, but again there was an air of embarrassment about the response. They turned down Dublin Street. 'How much longer have you got?'

'Eight weeks, I guess. All of a sudden it seems awful close.'

'Have you thought of names yet?'

Virginia shook her head, smiling. 'Saul doesn't want to. He says wait until after it arrives. Sometimes he's so superstitious, you know? Almost as if he's afraid something might go wrong . . .'

'That's understandable.' Liz's expression was hard to read. Suddenly Virginia felt an impulse of pity towards her. She put her hand on the other woman's arm.

'No luck yet, huh?' she said gently. 'With the baby, I mean . . .'

'Oh, we keep trying.' The note of reserve changed to one of forced cheerfulness. 'I'm sure it'll all come right in the end.'

'That's what I keep telling Saul.' Virginia hesitated, torn between loyalty to her husband and the desire to impart a confidence. 'The fact is, living with him hasn't been easy, these past few months. I don't think he was exactly delighted when I told him I was pregnant . . .' She was surprised at the effect her remark seemed to have on Liz.

The other woman flushed red. 'You mustn't think that,' she stammered. 'I'm sure . . . I mean, it's a difficult time . . .'

'Men get jealous, I know. I've read all those articles too. But with Saul I think there's something else . . .'

Liz was silent.

'It's not that he doesn't want the baby,' Virginia went on. 'I think he wants it as much as I do. It's just the timing's wrong. He has his thesis to finish and I was supposed to be getting my teaching diploma, you know?'

'Timing's all important,' said Liz sombrely. 'Believe me, I know.' She stopped outside the street door, fumbling for her keys. 'If there's anything we can do, Guy and me,' she said, 'you know we'd be only too happy. I mean, anything at all . . .'

'Why, thank you, that's really sweet,' Virginia said, a little mystified by this sudden access of emotion. Liz was nice, she thought, but maybe a little intense.

'Oh, Cathy,' Virginia stopped her in the hall one morning as she was getting ready to go out. 'I'm making lunch for all of us on Sunday. Just Saul and me and Liz and Guy. And you of course.'

'It sounds like a nice idea.'

'I thought you might like to bring someone. That nice boy you've been seeing . . .'

'Jonathan.' Catherine smiled, as if at some private joke. 'I'm sure he'd enjoy that.'

'It'll be like old times,' Virginia said. 'Making brunch for six. When we first got married, Saul and I used to entertain quite a bit. Believe it or not, he's a pretty good cook.'

'A man of many parts,' Catherine said.

★

'Of course, it's bound to come unstuck,' said Guy, waving his knife by way of emphasis. 'Those kind of arrangements always do. I can't see it lasting more than six months. A year at most.'

'The question is,' Jonathan murmured, 'is it a marriage of convenience or merely an illicit liaison?'

'Are we still talking about politics?' said Virginia. 'Only you make it sound so much more interesting . . . More coffee, anyone?'

'Jonathan can turn any subject to sex,' Catherine said sweetly.

'Guy's the same with politics.' Liz trickled maple syrup on to a piece of cinnamon toast. 'Gosh, Virginia, this is wonderful.'

There were murmurs of agreement around the table, where the three couples, seated according to Virginia's table-plan, so that no one was next to his or her partner, were enjoying a leisurely Sunday meal, at which the dishes had combined the eclecticism of breakfast with the substantiality of lunch. Grapefruit and cinnamon toast had been followed by scrambled eggs and smoked salmon. Jonathan had brought champagne.

It wasn't every day, Virginia said, looking at Saul, who was seated opposite her at the far end of the table, that they got the chance to return a little of the hospitality they had received. 'Everyone's been so nice. We're going to miss you all, aren't we, darling?'

'I'll make some more coffee,' said Saul, pushing back his chair.

'Are you planning to leave?' said Jonathan innocently.

'Well, not right away. But Saul's applied to lots of places back home, haven't you, darling? Cornell might be interested. Maybe Harvard. I guess it's just a matter of time before we hear something. Isn't it, Saul?'

'Nothing's settled yet,' said Saul.

146

'No, but we have to think of the future.' Virginia began stacking dishes. 'I mean, with the baby coming . . .'

'Nobody knows that better than I do. I just don't think we should assume anything.'

'Shall we go next door?' said Liz. 'It might be more comfortable. Virginia, leave the clearing up. You've done enough. Catherine and I can do it later . . .'

Sun streamed in through the big windows, illuminating the room in which they sat as if it were a stage set. A drawing-room comedy, Catherine thought. Jonathan had put on *Don Giovanni* and lay sprawling in an armchair, his eyes closed, listening to the music. Guy was reading the Sunday papers. Liz sat on the floor at his feet, resting her head against his knees. A pile of exercise books lay beside her, ready for marking. Saul had his arm around Virginia, who sat next to him on the sofa. No one spoke for a while. Catherine picked up a book.

> *Non sperar, se non m'uccidi,*
> *Ch'io ti lasci fuggir mai!*

'God, I feel sleepy,' said Virginia. 'That glass of champagne really knocked me out.'

> *Donna folle! indarno gridi,*
> *Chi son io tu non saprai!*

'Go to sleep then.' Saul shifted his position to accommodate her warm, drowsy body. He looked over at Catherine, curled up on the window-seat. She glanced up from the book she was attempting to read and yawned. Catching his eye, she turned the yawn into an elaborate stretch, arching her body like a cat's. Their next meeting was arranged for the following afternoon. He didn't know if he could wait that long.

Gente! Servi! Al traditore!

'What a charming domestic scene,' Jonathan murmured. 'A picture of marital bliss. I suppose you and I are the only renegades,' he said to Catherine. 'Doesn't it make you feel we're missing something?'

Taci e trema al mio furore!

'You'll be surprised,' Virginia said sleepily, her eyes closed. 'One day the right person will come along.'

Scellerato!

'Do you really think so? How exciting. I can hardly wait,' said Jonathan.

Sconsigliata!

'Interesting piece here on the Lib-Lab pact,' said Guy.

'I don't know how you can bear it.' Liz stood at the sink, up to her elbows in soapy water. In her agitation, she washed and re-washed the same plate. 'Seeing her every day and getting to know her and hearing about the baby and . . . and . . .'

'Sleeping with her husband,' said Catherine. She took the clean plate out of Liz's hands and began to dry it.

'Precisely,' said Liz. 'I don't know how you can do it.'

'It's not so difficult.'

'What I mean is, I don't know how you can bring yourself to do it. To lie to her . . .'

'You get used to it,' said Catherine. 'After a while, it doesn't feel like lying.'

'Whatever it feels like, it's dishonest.' Liz spoke with sudden passion, the wine glass she was in the process of washing forgotten in her hand. 'It was different before she came. What you and Saul got up to was your own affair. But now . . . I feel involved. We both do.'

'Are you going to tell her?' The question hung unanswered in the air, as Liz drained and wiped the sink and took off her apron.

Saul put his head round the door of the kitchen. 'Anything I can do?' he said.

'All finished,' Liz said, a touch sharply. 'Don't worry,' she said to Catherine, 'I feel compromised enough as it is. I won't do your dirty work for you.'

IO

The city in midsummer was a place of shifting populations, a meeting place of transients. Americans, Japanese, Italians thronged the streets. It was impossible to walk anywhere without being asked for directions. The city's carnival mood, always at its height in August, was exacerbated, that year, by the Jubilee festivities. People got themselves up in absurd costumes, transformed themselves, with the aid of make-up and props, into pantomime figures. It was as if the whole country were engaged in some bizarre re-enactment of history, raiding a collective dressing-up box for cast-offs.

Of the student population, most had migrated elsewhere for the duration of the summer. Only a few lingered in the city, aimless spirits, held by poverty or obsession. Catherine was amongst them. Her professed reason for remaining was her intention of finishing the first draft of her thesis. She had rejected offers from the Urquharts to share their cottage in the Highlands, from the Orrs to accompany them to Florence and from Jonathan Strange to visit him at his parents' home in Brighton. The Meyers, too, remained. Virginia had passed the seventh month of her pregnancy, after which she had been advised not to travel long distances by air, and Saul, in any case, had reasons of his own for staying on. His work was the reason he gave.

That summer Catherine's life settled into a regular pattern of lies and evasions. As the weeks passed she found herself becoming increasingly comfortable with deceit, so much so, in fact, that she was able to convince herself that she was behaving rather well. No shade of malice or resentment coloured her demeanour towards Virginia. She was, in all respects but one, perfectly open with her. Her openness, she knew, was her best disguise.

Her meetings with Saul took place in Jonathan Strange's rooms, a few minutes' walk from the London Street flat. It was, despite Saul's initial misgivings, a convenient arrangement, requiring only a slight deviation from the accustomed route home from the university. In the drab surroundings of Warrender Park Road their encounters had seemed furtive, squalid; the handsome nineteenth-century apartment in Circus Place, by contrast, imparted an operatic quality to their affair, as if they were rehearsing scenes from *La Traviata*. In its spaciousness and in the masculine austerity with which it was furnished, the flat was reminiscent of a set of rooms in a Cambridge college, an impression heightened by the few possessions – steel engravings of Roman views, an edition of Ruskin's *Complete Works* bound in faded green calfskin – provided by its current occupant.

Jonathan's sitting room, with its worn leather sofa, its regency striped wallpaper faded to the colour of an old bloodstain, its writing desk, once the property of a doctor, which still bore on its scarred leather top the imprint of hastily blotted prescriptions, seemed the perfect setting for their bourgeois-bohemian affair. A similar opulence could be discerned in the bedroom furnishings, where the solid Edwardian comfort of mahogany bedstead and walnut chest of drawers, of ormolu pier-glass and marble-topped washstand, was offset by the austerity of white walls and brown holland blinds. Over the bed Jonathan had hung a nineteenth-century print of Poussin's *Et in Arcadia Ego*.

'What's it like, having sex with her?'

'Jesus, Catherine. Give me a break . . .'

'Come on. I want to know. It must be strange, doing it with a pregnant woman.'

'It's not so strange. You just adapt.' He had an image, as he spoke, of Virginia's body, heavy and round as a ripe pear as she knelt over him, his light thrusts just parting the soft lips of her sex. Making love to her these last weeks had been a kind of Zen exercise, requiring a degree of erotic control he hadn't known, till then, he possessed.

'Do you enjoy it?'

'I thought we agreed, no questions about that.'

'I didn't agree to anything. So do you?'

'For God's sake. We don't even do it that much, since she got so big . . .'

'You did it last night. I heard you.'

'Come *on* . . .'

'I can't help it if the walls in that place are thin. Well, are you going to tell me or not?'

'Tell you what?'

'Which of us you like better in bed.'

'That's easy. You, of course.'

'Liar.'

'Would I lie to you?'

'Why not? It must get to be second nature, after a while . . .'

'I have to go.'

'Now I've hurt your feelings.'

'It takes a lot more than that. I was just thinking maybe you're getting jealous. All these questions . . .'

'Don't flatter yourself. I just like to know what's going on.'

'Including my sex-life.'

'Especially your sex-life.'

'I really do have to go.' Saul made no attempt to move however. They were lying in bed, watching the light shift round from one side of Jonathan's room to the other. It was half past five, the beginning of a long midsummer evening. Saul was meeting his wife and in-laws for drinks before the theatre. The Kellys had arrived a few days before and were staying at a small hotel in Regent Terrace. They were indefatigable tourists, arriving early each morning to collect their daughter for sightseeing trips and taking in a different play or film every evening. Saul had avoided most of these excursions, pleading pressure of work, but that night, after the theatre, his father-in-law had booked a table at a new French restaurant in Rose Street to celebrate the imminent arrival of his first grandchild.

'Go on then.'

'I'd rather stay here with you.'

'And disappoint Virginia? Besides, I thought you liked Chekhov.'

'I'm not in the mood for him right now . . .' He kissed her smooth warm shoulders, her throat, her mouth, her eyes.

'You'd better hurry,' said Catherine, 'or you'll miss the first act.'

Reluctantly he got up and went through to the bathroom, a room in which the furnishings displayed the same otiose grandeur as those in the rest of the apartment. The taps were solid brass, the lavatory seat a slab of mahogany. 'Hey, guess what?' he called, over the sound of running water. 'The King is dead. Long live the King.'

'I know. I heard it on the radio. Isn't it sad?'

'He had it coming. All that sex, drugs and booze.' He returned after a few minutes, his hair damp, and began to dress, crooning a few bars of 'Heartbreak Hotel' under his breath.

When he had gone she moved around the borrowed flat, erasing traces of their temporary occupancy of the place. Smoothing rumpled sheets, picking up damp towels. Her task completed, she sat for a while in Jonathan's sitting room, smoking a cigarette. She had drawn the shutters against the sun and a single band of bright gold drew its narrow diagonal across the floor, bisecting carpet, faded wallpaper, Roman print. The air had a musty, evocative scent, a compound of old books, dust and furniture polish. In that moment she saw the place for what it was: an ante-chamber, a waiting room. It seemed to her then that her life had been no more than a series of such rooms, each furnished with the relics of futile exchanges.

★

Saul arrived at the theatre a little after six-thirty to find his wife and in-laws waiting for him in the upstairs bar. As he climbed the staircase – an ornate double sweep, like the setting for a dance routine in a Hollywood musical comedy of the 1930s – he could hear his father-in-law in the middle of telling a story, his mother-in-law's tinkling laugh. Nervously he checked his appearance in the mirror over the bar for signs of debauchery. His tie was crooked; otherwise, he was a model of propriety.

'. . . so I said to the guy, what do you mean it's already been chilled? I'm drinking the stuff and if I say it's not cold enough it's not cold enough! Back home we like our food hot and our drinks cold. Here it seems to be the other way around . . .'

'Oh, Daddy, you didn't . . .'

'I certainly did. You should have seen the guy's face.'

'Here's Saul,' said Mrs Kelly, making room for him. 'Why don't you get him a drink, Jack? The poor boy looks exhausted.' Her narrow eyes, the same colour as Virginia's, scrutinized him thoughtfully.

Saul felt the blood rise to his face. 'I forgot the time,' he said. 'I had to run.'

'I guess you must've been working too hard,' said Marie Kelly, patting his hand.

'Don't talk to me about Saul's work,' Virginia said with a petulant shrug. 'Sometimes I get the feeling that's all he cares about.'

'Now, Virginia, don't give the poor boy a hard time.' Marie threw him a flirtatious look. 'You know he's only doing it for you and the baby.' She was looking very pretty, Saul thought, seeing in her fine-drawn features and dark hair lightly touched with grey a vision of Virginia in twenty years' time.

'If there's not enough ice in your Scotch, just shout,' said Jack, returning with the drinks. 'They seem to have a problem here with ice. I can't understand why. It doesn't cost anything.'

'It's the principle of it,' said Saul. 'The British like their drinks warm.'

'No wonder the country's going down the tubes. I mean, without the tourist industry to support it this place would be on a hiding to nowhere, right? Not that things are much better back home. Did you see what that jerk Carter said the other day? He wants us all to drive smaller cars. I mean, first he wrecks our nuclear program and now he wants Americans to drive small cars. Is the guy *crazy*, or what?'

'Oh, don't start talking politics,' said Marie. 'Tell us about this play we're going to see, Saul.'

'The girl at the Festival office said it was a comedy,' said Jack. 'Is it funny?'

'Oh, come on,' said Marie. 'It's Chekhov. Chekhov isn't funny.'

'It all depends on your point of view,' said Saul.

'It'd better be funny,' said Jack darkly.

The lights went up on the dark stage. A burst of laughter greeted Masha's famous first line. Out of the corner of his eye Saul saw his father-in-law's bemused shrug and grinned to himself. As the play within the play began, his thoughts returned to his own situation. Sometimes he thought there must be an element of perversity in his make-up. He had everything going for him. Career prospects. A loving wife. It was what he had wanted, what he had worked for – all his life. Then why did he have the impulse to throw it all away?

'Are you okay?' Virginia touched his hand in the dark.

'Sure I'm okay,' he murmured, conscious of the hissing injunctions to silence from the Chekhov lovers in the row behind.

'Talk to me later.'

He focused his attention on the play. The darkened garden. The makeshift stage. A man and a woman talking about art. The actress playing Nina was a beauty, Saul observed. Her lover, Trepliov – a tall, handsome boy obviously cast for his resemblance to the young Chekhov – clearly thought so. There was an element of sexual tension which made the scenes between them electrifying. Saul found himself, suddenly, following the action as if its outcome held the solution to his own dilemma. The characters on stage seemed emanations of his own consciousness. Trepliov the nihilist, unlucky in love. Trigorin the cynic, using all the sophistry at his command to get a girl into bed, but caring for nothing but his work. His precious fictions. *A subject for a short story*. That was his life alright.

'What I don't understand is why he killed himself,' Virginia said as they walked back along Royal Terrace, after leaving the Kellys at their hotel. 'It was obvious she wasn't worth it. She couldn't have the guy she wanted, so she wrecked the other guy's life instead . . .'

'Uh huh,' said Saul. He felt light-headed, the effect of the champagne he had drunk that evening perhaps.

'Women like that — ' His wife broke off her exposition. 'You're not listening, are you? You don't care what I think . . .'

'Sure I care. I just had too much to drink, that's all.'

'Are you getting one of your migraines?'

'I told you, I feel fine.' The memory of Nina and Trepliov's last scene together made him tremble. The bad actress and the failed writer, drawn together into the whirlpool. When they embraced for the last time, he had felt his eyes burn with tears.

'Only you were so quiet all evening I thought something must be wrong. Is it my parents? I know Daddy can be a little hard to take sometimes, but . . .'

'It's nothing to do with your parents. Your parents are fine.'

'Is it me?' she said in a small voice.

'Of course not.'

'Sometimes I think' – her voice cracked into tears – 'you're mad at me. Or tired of me. Or both.'

'I'm not tired of you.'

He put his arm round her shoulder as together, in the strange midsummer twilight, they descended the precipitous street.

Nights in midsummer were as white as days. It never seemed to get dark. At midnight the streets were thronged with revellers on their way to parties. In the half-light they had no shadows, like the undead.

Catherine went to a party one night in the Botanical Gardens. When she arrived at about eleven the sun was still shining in a cloudless sky. People were smoking and drinking wine from paper cups and there was a distant sound of music. Behind its locked gates the place had a deserted, magical feel. In the ornamental borders red and orange flowers burned like swords.

There was no one at the party she knew. The boy who had invited her, an acquaintance run into at an earlier party, had disappeared, leaving her stranded. For the first time in months she felt herself free of obligations. There was no one here she had to talk to. No one in front of whom she would have to watch what she said. She sat on a fallen pillar in a neo-classical garden and talked to a fish-farmer from Loch Gilpead. There was a smell of cut grass, night-scented flowers and marijuana. Around them dancers wove intricate parabolas on the grass, like figures in a masque.

Towards Saul her feelings were becoming increasingly ambivalent. What had started as a straightforward sexual involvement was becoming more complicated. She found her emotions engaged, more than she would have liked. A straightforward involvement. The phrase was itself a contradiction in terms. Implicit in most of the words describing sexual relations was an element of tortuousness, Catherine thought. Entanglement. Liaison. It was no accident that love's emblem took the form of a knot.

'Sometimes I find myself longing – really longing – for oblivion,' she told Alasdair, whose whisky she was drinking.

'What a funny girl you are,' he said thoughtfully. He smiled at her. His eyes were brown, she noticed. She liked brown eyes. He seemed to like her, even though she was talking nonsense.

What's the matter with me? thought Catherine. If I had any sense I'd let this nice man take me home. 'The trouble with me is, I'm not serious about anything,' she said. 'That's why my life's such a mess.'

'I can't believe that,' said Alasdair seriously. 'You're just unhappy. Do you want to tell me about it?'

'Maybe later,' said Catherine, thinking with shame of all the times she'd told the story of her life to strange men at parties. 'I feel like dancing. Let's dance.'

11

The afternoon Virginia found the letter was one of an unbroken chain of perfect days. Cloudless sky. Warm golden light. A distant murmur of thunder.

She had been resting and awoke suddenly with the feeling that someone had spoken: low, distinct tones conveyed an urgent message which, on opening her eyes, she could not recall. She lay for a while, too exhausted to move. As if at a given signal, the child inside her began to move. A series of powerful kicks and squirming motions were visible, as she watched, beneath the tightly stretched skin of her abdomen.

'Oh, be quiet,' she said crossly, in the room's silence. She knew without looking at her watch that she had overslept. In an hour – perhaps less, to judge from the angle of the shadows – Saul would be home, expecting a meal. Lying there, like some beached aquatic creature, she considered without enthusiasm the small tasks that lay ahead. Chopping vegetables. Preparing steaks. Even the little effort required by these activities seemed too great. Sighing, Virginia heaved herself upright. The sweat ran down her back as she bent to retrieve her dropped bathrobe and, as she straightened, she felt a roaring of pressure in her ears.

Running her bath, she saw that the bottle of scented oil Saul had brought her from the drugstore last week was missing. Probably Catherine had taken it – it would be just like her to borrow someone else's things without asking. Virginia padded barefoot across the hall to reclaim what was hers.

Catherine's personality impressed itself upon the room in a number of oblique ways: creases left by her absent form on the unmade bed, dust on the mirror, clothes strewn on the floor. A heap of shoes – spike-heeled pumps, roman sandals, purple leather boots – lay like the discarded external skeletons of some soft-bodied creature. A handful of shells, picked up on a winter's walk along the seashore and carried around for a month or two in a coat pocket, had been deposited without arrangement on the dressing-table, amongst a wreckage of dried-up tubes of make-up and broken necklaces. The missing bottle of rose-scented oil was amongst them. Virginia took it and turned to go. It was then that she saw the letter. Not at first realizing what it was she saw.

On the floor by the bed, half-hidden by a paperback copy of *Tender Is the Night*, a note in her husband's distinctive, sloping hand caught her eye. After no more than a moment's hesitation she picked it up, leaving the book where it was. She read it almost before the first, startled moment of recognition was past. The implications of what it said took somewhat longer to assimilate.

Can't make it tonight. Something's come up. How about tomorrow? Usual time. S.

There was no date, nothing by which she could fix the thing in context, explain it away. She searched her memory for a conversation, a reference to a change of plan – anything which would serve as a commentary on this puzzlingly elliptical message – and came up with nothing conclusive. *Something's come up.* There'd been an evening a couple of weeks back, when her parents were visiting. She'd been going to accompany them to the opera. A new production of *Carmen*. But at the last moment, she'd felt too tired. Saul had been intending, he said, to work late at the library, but had decided to stay home with her instead. They'd had a quiet evening, gone to bed early. But why, if that was indeed what Saul's note alluded to, should these things concern Catherine?

How about tomorrow? Usual time.

It was the suggestion of something habitual – *Usual time* – which gave the letter its air of clandestine intimacy. And yet, after all, it might be possible to explain it away. It could mean anything, or nothing. Virginia read the note through again, before replacing it as nearly as possible in the position in which she had found it. She stood for a minute, irresolute, in the long, narrow room flooded with golden light, with the sensation that she was seeing everything for the first time. Shapes of objects seemed more sharply defined, colours brighter. So bright they seemed unreal, Virginia thought.

For the next few days the letter was a source of irritation in Virginia's consciousness, an inflamed spot she could not stop herself from picking at. *Can't make it tonight.* Each phrase, as she probed it for meaning, seemed loaded with power to harm. And yet, at the same time, there seemed nothing in it. If, as one interpretation suggested, the letter spelled betrayal, why had it been so inexpertly concealed – or rather, not concealed at all – as if its contents were blameless? And yet, and yet. Unable to leave it alone, she delved beneath the skin. Scratched it until it began to bleed. *How about tomorrow?* The question concealed a barb. Implicit in its reference to an unknown tomorrow was a succession of tomorrows. A complicity.

Virginia observed her husband, alone and in company, for signs of alteration, but found none. His attentiveness towards her neither diminished nor increased, although sometimes it seemed to her he was aware of her scrutiny. Once or twice he had asked her what was on her mind, but teasingly, as if secure in the knowledge of his own invulnerability.

'What are you thinking about, sweetheart?'

'Nothing. Why?'

'No reason at all. Love me?'

'You know I do.'

There were times when she thought him transparent. Incapable of guile. Others when she was not so sure. In his dealings with Catherine he was scrupulous to a fault, Virginia observed. No shadow of ambiguity was allowed to cloud their conversation which – at least when she was around – was confined to neutral topics, brief exchanges of information. Although there were occasions when Virginia thought she intercepted something – a look, an intonation – which might have held some questionable shade of meaning. It might have been no more than her imagination. A trick of the light.

It was September, season of dying falls. People were drifting back after the university vacation. Itinerant populations of actors and tourists moved on. One day, without warning, it rained. Hard, heavy pellets cracked into the white dust on the sidewalk and rustled the dry leaves of trees in Princes Street gardens. There was a sharp smell of wet grass.

Saul ran into Magda in Dublin Street. She was brown from a Long Island summer. Looking at her gleaming limbs, her sun-darkened face, made him feel pallid, washed up. His First Draft, completed after weeks of effort, seemed a dull-witted thing, not worth the anguish it had cost him. An analogy suggested itself to him between the bundles of notes and spoiled drafts on which all summer he had struggled to impose an order and the untidy contingencies of his life. In both a structure lay concealed, if only he could find it.

'So how was your summer?' Magda said. 'You didn't spend it all in libraries, I hope?'

It seemed to him that that was exactly what he had done, hiding from the sun behind the closed blinds of the faculty building, or in the shuttered darkness of the room on Circus Place. His affair with Catherine drifted on. Shapeless. Meaningless. His marriage was a sham. 'It was okay, I guess. Virginia's parents came over.'

'What a drag.'

'It wasn't too bad really.' At least it had kept Virginia happy, he thought. Since Jack and Marie had left, she'd been unpredictable in her moods, given to sudden outbursts of tears or hysterical laughter.

'How *is* Virginia?'

164

'Fine. Bigger, of course.'

'Poor thing. She must hate it. God, I hope I never get pregnant,' said Magda with a shudder. She looked at him slyly. 'Are you still seeing Catherine? Okay, okay, don't answer that. Hey, almost forgot.' With a delicacy which was uncharacteristic of her, Magda changed the subject. 'I'm having a party on the eighth. To mark the beginning of my fourth decade. God, it makes me feel so old. Everything's got this kind of *fin de siècle* feel. Like I was kissing my youth goodbye . . .'

'I know just how you feel.'

'Oh, *you*. You're nothing but a baby,' Magda said scornfully. 'Don't forget, will you? Characters in fiction.'

He stared at her.

'The theme of my party,' she said.

Saul was rewriting his chapter on *The Masque of Cupid*. Spenser and the dark workings of his allegory had never seemed so compelling. Here was form and meaning in abundance. An elegant grid of symmetries to place upon disorder.

'I mean, what am I going to *wear*, for heaven's sake?'

Virginia's voice disrupted his thoughts on the significance of the bleeding heart in the silver dish, one of the poem's more ambiguous images. *At that wide orifice her trembling hart/Was drawne forth, and in silver basin laid* . . . There was something disturbingly sexual, even sado-masochistic, about the image.

'Did you say something?' He made a note in the margin: *cf. Baudelaire, Mon Coeur Mis à Nu*, then put down his pen with a look of mild reproof. 'Only I have to finish this paper . . .'

'You have no idea how difficult it is to find a pregnant character in fiction. I know. I checked. There's no shortage of women having abortions, women dying in childbirth and pregnant women killing themselves. I guess it goes without saying . . .'

'Angel . . .'

'. . . because most writers are men.'

'Oh come *on*. What about Jane Austen? Or . . . or Virginia Woolf. Terrific writers . . .'

'A lot they knew about being pregnant.' All at once tears overflowed from Virginia's large blue eyes and rolled down her cheeks in slow dignified streams. He got up and put his arms around her.

'Gina, baby, what's the matter?' There was an edge of impatience beneath his solicitude. This was not the first time she had demanded his attention with an emotional outburst. He wondered what it was he'd said or done. 'Is it the heat? Your blood pressure maybe? You know Mr Forster said you had to be careful . . .'

'Oh Saul . . .' She pulled away from him with an angry shake of the shoulders. 'Don't you ever listen? Just for one *second*? I'm talking about this damn party . . .'

'Party?' He looked at her. Then he understood. 'You mean that thing of Magda's? I can't believe you're letting yourself get so upset about it.'

'It's all right for you to laugh,' she said furiously. 'You don't have this problem of what to wear. "Characters in fiction" – what sort of dumb idea is that? Well, just *look* at me!' She blew her nose. 'I can't exactly disguise it, can I?'

'I guess not. Hey, look, it doesn't matter that much. Some stupid party. If you feel that bad about it, we don't have to go . . .'

'I want to go.' She leaned her head against him. Her flushed and gleaming face, beneath its mass of damp curls, seemed too heavy for the slender neck.

'So we'll go. I'll think of something. What about Lawrence? Isn't there some scene in one of his books where . . .'

'Sure. Anna. *The Rainbow*. She dances naked, for Christ's sake. I don't think it's that kind of party.'

'You never can tell.' He saw her face. 'Oh come on, angel, it was a joke . . .'

'It's just I hate being like this.' She was crying again. 'So

166

ugly . . . so *gross*. It feels like everybody's staring at me, when I walk down the street.'

'You know that's not true.' He stroked her wet face, murmuring words of consolation. But in his mind's eye he saw the fine, painted mask of his lover; a reminder, if he needed it, of his duplicity.

The party was in full swing when they arrived at Magda's. From the street could be heard the pulsing of music. Coloured lights flashed on and off in the first-floor windows.The door was opened by an unshaven, barefoot man in a stained white T-shirt and dirty jeans, low-slung beneath his bulging belly.

'Don't tell me – let me guess,' said Saul. 'Jack Kerouac on a bad night.'

Donald gave him an ugly look. 'Who's your friend?' he said to Virginia.

She smiled at him from behind her black velvet mask. 'Hi Donald.'

Magda appeared, already a little drunk. She kissed her newly arrived guests. 'Donald refuses to be a character in fiction,' she complained loudly. 'Isn't it typical?'

'I prefer to be a character in my own fiction,' Donald said with dignity, 'and leave the rest of you to your charades.'

'Don't mind him,' said Magda. 'He's upset because his publisher turned down his latest book. Virginia, you look fabulous. Who are you, anyway? The Dark Lady?'

'No,' said Virginia. 'But close . . .'

'Have you guessed who I am yet?' said Magda, displaying her own costume, a high waisted, hobble-skirted gown with a generous décolletage. 'I'll give you a clue. She's a famous adulterer.'

'That narrows it down I guess,' said Saul.

'Magda, answer the door for fuck's sake. They've been ringing for ten minutes,' bellowed Donald from the kitchen.

'Drinks in there, food in there, coats in the bedroom,' said Magda distractedly, hurrying to obey this injunction.

'Are you okay for a minute while I fetch the drinks?' Saul said to his wife, who stood looking at herself in the mirror in Magda's bedroom. The heavy brocade gown with its slashed sleeves and bodice sewn with fake pearls and glass emeralds transformed her body into an unyielding shape. A painted doll, he thought. The enormous skirts, which hid her advanced state of pregnancy, constrained her to walk with little, gliding steps, as if she were on wheels.

'I'm perfectly fine. You have lipstick on your cheek,' she said, licking her finger to wipe it away.

In the kitchen Donald was talking to Marcel Proust. 'The novel. What do any of them know about the novel?' he was saying morosely. 'They wouldn't know a good novel if it got up and kicked them in the balls.'

'You could always try another publisher,' murmured Proust.

Saul recognized the voice as Jonathan Strange's. He had to admit the disguise was a good one. In his black frock coat, black and grey striped trousers, white shirt-front and black cravat, his hair darkened with brilliantine, his full red lips partially concealed beneath a waxed moustache, he looked the very image of the youthful nineties dandy, in the days before asthma and literary endeavour seduced him away from the Faubourg Saint-Germain.

'Maybe,' Donald agreed, filling his glass. 'But in my experience they're all as bad as each other. Money. That's all they understand. Oh Christ, if it isn't the Demon King,' he said rudely, noticing Saul.

'Is there any orange juice?' Saul said mildly, ignoring this provocation. 'My wife can't take alcohol.'

'It *is* you,' Jonathan said with his lazy, faintly insolent smile. 'I wondered for a minute. Who are you meant to be? Hamlet, I suppose.'

'God, they all fancy themselves as Hamlet,' Donald jeered. 'That self-absorbed prat . . .'

'I'm not Hamlet.'

Donald paid no attention to this protest. 'Look at them,' he said loudly, sweeping his arm out to include the other occupants of the room. 'A bunch of self-absorbed prats making even bigger prats of themselves. You'd think they had better things to do than play dressing-up, wouldn't you? Wankers.'

'Dear old Donald, such an uncompromising realist,' said Jonathan with a little shudder. He looked at Saul. '*Love* the tights,' he drawled. 'Of course, you've got the legs for it.'

It would be satisfying to hit him, Saul thought.

'Why don't you see if you can find Albertine?' Jonathan fanned himself with his white kid gloves. His predatory gaze moved from Saul's legs to a young man got up as Satan in gold body-paint and cardboard wings.

'Albertine?' Saul stared at the lounging, insouciant figure.

'Your *petite amie*,' the other yawned, 'or rather mine. But you can have her, just for tonight. She's around somewhere. Looking quite delectable, if you like that sort of thing.'

'Thanks,' said Saul.

'My pleasure,' Jonathan said, smoothing back his hair with a long white hand.

In the big drawing room the difficulty of finding his lover in the crowd was compounded by the mirrors which ran from floor to ceiling down one side of the room, doubling its size and the number of people in it. Reflections of reflections, Saul thought, scanning the crowd for a face he knew. Around him miscellaneous characters in search of an author were dancing. Jay Gatsby and Daisy. Hans Castorp and Clavdia Chauchat. Some of the pairs, either by accident or design, were ill-matched. Romeo was dancing with Emma Bovary, Don Juan with Clarissa Harlowe. In the corner, Joseph K was rolling a joint.

'Of course, it's an awful poem,' Saul heard a familiar voice say, 'but that's not the point.' The speaker's air of fastidious pedantry was intensified by his costume, a close-fitting, high-necked tunic which gave him the look of a pale-faced *apparatchik*. He was wearing *pince-nez*. 'Once you let the bigots win, where's it going to stop? The implications are frightening . . .'

'First they burn books, then they burn people,' said a woman in black.

'Hey,' said Saul. 'It's you. I didn't recognize you.'

'That's the general idea isn't it?' said Catherine. 'Sweet of you to bring me some wine.' She took a sip from the glass and handed it back to him.

'You can keep it. The orange juice is for Virginia. Have you seen her?'

'It's hard to say. Who is she?'

'Helena in *All's Well*. The only pregnant woman in Shakespeare.'

'Perhaps she sees you as Bertram. A heartless shit,' Catherine said.

'Don't think I haven't thought of it. I like your dress.'

'I think it makes me look suitably depraved, don't you?' Of the various images available to her on which to model the character of Albertine, she had rejected that of the incandescent girl on the beach at Balbec for the enchantress of *Sodome et Gomorrhe*. Her black velvet dress, tight at the waist, left her arms and the upper part of her breasts bare. Diamanté earrings sparkled amongst the dark curls of false hair, arranged in a chignon at the nape of her neck. Her lips were a deep carmine and on her cheekbone was a single beauty spot, like the blemish on a rosepetal.

'Definitely,' said Saul.

'We were discussing the *Gay News* trial,' Robin Orr said coldly. 'I don't know what your views are, but . . .'

'Oh, I try not to have views,' said Saul. He looked at Catherine. 'I have to talk to you.'

'I almost forgot,' Robin said. 'I've got something for you.'

He handed Saul a slim volume, bound in matt black. 'My latest work.'

'Interesting title,' Saul said.

'Glad you approve. It was Gillian's idea to make it two words, instead of one. In fidelity, you see. Like *In Memoriam*. A shade more ambivalent, don't you think?'

'Oh absolutely.' Saul opened the book. The first poem was called, simply, 'Party'. He read a few lines, then closed the book. 'Are they all like the first one?' he said.

A smile flickered briefly across Robin's lips and was quenched. 'They deal with similar themes, yes. That's the whole point. It's a sequence.'

'I thought it was rather good,' said Catherine, 'but then it isn't every day I get a book dedicated to me.'

Saul flipped open the cover. *For Catherine – in fidelity*.

'Isn't it a little indiscreet?' he said.

'Oh, it's quite usual,' Robin said. 'I can write your name in, if you like.'

'I think I'd rather you didn't,' Saul said.

'Rather he didn't what?' said Virginia, encircling his waist from behind.

'Hey,' he said. 'Where did you get to?'

'What a wonderful costume,' Catherine said. The other woman grimaced.

'It's a little hot.' She took the book of poems from Saul's hand. 'What's this?' she said. She opened it and read, '"Garden of Earthly Delights"'. That's a great title.'

'Thank you,' said Robin. 'Unfortunately it's not mine. I wish it were.'

'Did you write it? But that's terrific.' She read a few lines aloud.

'There's no need to embarrass him,' said Saul.

'Oh, I'm quite used to having my work read in public,' Robin said airily.

'Well I think it's great,' said Virginia. 'Can I borrow it?'

'It's a gift,' Robin said. 'To both of you.'

They were joined by Gillian. Her dress, which was dark grey and of severe cut, suggested the nunnery or the school-room. The only decorative touch was a gilt crucifix, worn at her throat. 'Good God,' she said loudly. 'Who *are* all these people?'

'Friends of Magda's, one imagines,' said Robin.

'I can't think where she finds them all,' she said crossly. 'I suppose we might as well dance.'

'He looks like Rasputin in that get-up,' said Saul, watching them go.

'Raskolnikov,' said Catherine. 'I think it rather suits him.'

'Why don't you two dance?' said Virginia.

Saul looked dubious. 'I don't think so,' he said.

'Go on,' said Virginia. 'You know you love dancing.'

'What about you?' Catherine said.

Virginia made a face. 'You have to be kidding. I can hardly walk, let alone dance.'

'I don't mind.' Catherine looked at Saul. He shook his head. A warning look, which Virginia intercepted. It was that look, she thought afterwards, which convinced her of his guilt. It said, as plainly as if he had spoken, *Not here. Not now.*

'I'll be fine, really,' she said, seating herself in a corner of the window-seat. 'I'll just sit here and read some of Robin's poems.'

'It's too dark to read,' said Saul.

When she saw her husband dancing with Catherine Marlowe, Virginia knew she had been betrayed. The realization grew until it was as much as she could do to remain where she was and not run from the room, away from the knowing or amused looks of those who were aware of her humiliation, as well as from those who had caused it. The music, a slow ballad with mournful lyrics extolling the pleasures of erotic annihilation, was of the sort to encourage proximity. Yet Saul was as far away from his partner as it was possible to be and still hold her. It was as if she were made of glass and might break if he made a wrong move. Virginia observed his expression of relief as the music came to an end. The way his hand lingered, a fraction longer than was polite, in the small of Catherine's back as, released from the subtle torment of dancing, they made their way back through the crowd towards her.

She took refuge in the bedroom, where, amongst piles of coats, discarded wigs and cardboard swords, she considered what she was going to do. Her thoughts seemed to have entered a state of suspension, a false tranquillity, as if she were observing things from a great distance. When, some time later, she returned to the room where she had watched her husband dancing with his lover to find them locked in an unambiguous embrace, it seemed only the confirmation of something she already knew. An irrelevance, almost. She went away before they could come up for air.

Saul and Catherine stood watching the dancers. The room was now very full. It was no longer possible to make out the identity of the characters, as it had been earlier. A general confusion prevailed. Some of those invited had, in any case, chosen to interpret Magda's stipulation in its broadest sense, their costumes designating unease or dissatisfaction with the notion of character itself. Amongst this group were those who bore a family resemblance to the enigmatic figures of Beckettian theatre. They were dressed, without exception, in black. One said she was in mourning for the death of the novel. Another called himself a signifier without a sign.

'What a lot of people Magda knows,' said Catherine.

'It's her birthday. These people are her past.'

'Are we her past too, do you think?'

'Of course. Why else would she invite us? We represent significant moments in Magda's life. People she's slept with. People she hasn't slept with.'

'Emotional baggage . . .'

'Jettisoned along the way. That's how she manages to travel so light.' Saul drained his glass.

'I'm not sure I like being emotional baggage.'

'Listen,' he said, 'I've been thinking. We could go away. London maybe. Or back to the States.'

'Don't be absurd.'

'I mean it. What have we got to lose?'

Robin arrived, carrying drinks. 'Your wife's in the kitchen,' he told Saul. 'She seems a bit out of sorts.'

Saul gulped his wine with guilty haste, conscious of his unkind neglect. 'Excuse me a minute,' he said.

'With pleasure.' Robin turned to Catherine. 'Dance?' he said.

A dishevelled Molly Bloom was sitting on the kitchen table, showing off her legs. She put her arms round Saul's neck and blew smoke in his face. 'Want some?' she said throatily, offering him a joint.

'Not right now. I'm looking for Virginia.'

'She went to lie down.' She tightened her hold. 'Did anyone ever tell you you have a sexy mouth? If Donald wasn't the jealous type I'd . . .'

'I have to find her.' He disentangled himself from her pungent embrace.

In the bedroom a solemn group sat on the floor, passing a joint around.

'The thing about reality is, it's unreal,' said one. There was no sign of his wife. He tried the handle of the next room and a voice told him to go away.

'Hey, neat,' said a voice he knew. 'The Prince of Denmark, right? Can you guess who I am? I'll give you a clue . . .'

'I don't have time right now, Robert . . .'

'Henry James. Late period. *Live all you can*. Come on, man, it's easy . . .'

The door of the bathroom opened and Virginia came out.

174

On her white face twin circles of rouge glowed with the hard lustre of enamel.

'Where were you? I was looking for you all over,' said Saul with the indignation of one who is in the wrong.

'It was too hot for me in there. All that noise gave me a headache. I'm going home.'

'Oh, but you can't go yet,' cried Robert gallantly. 'Carol and I only just got here.'

'I'll go with you,' said Saul.

'No.' Her eyes held the brilliant shimmer of tears. 'You stay. No need for us both to miss the party.'

'I'll call a cab.'

'I already did.' She was fastening her cloak. Saul hesitated. Then the doorbell went, a strident, warped note. 'That'll be him now.'

'I won't be late,' he said.

Catherine stood on the balcony looking down into the street. The long windows of the mirrored room stood open behind her, affording glimpses of dancing shapes. Below her, as she looked towards Leith, she could see the lights of the New Town. The night air felt cool on her face, drying the sweat at her hairline beneath the fringe of false curls. She half closed her eyes, so that the lights of the city blurred into a mesh of interconnecting lines, a grid of stars.

The trouble with confusing life and art, Catherine thought, is that you find it hard to recognize the real thing when you see it. Life becomes tainted with the devices, the second-hand perceptions of art. Accustomed to defining her experience in terms of a set of fictional structures, she now found the structures inadequate. But what else was there? She'd yet to work that one out.

There was a hoarse shout in the street. A group of youths were walking in the centre of the road. One had caught sight of her, a dark shape against the pulsing red light of the room behind. She raised her hand in ironic salute and he fell on his knees with a groan.

'I want to fuck you,' he shouted.

It was the most honest proposal she had heard all night.

In the mirrored room the mood of the party had shifted. Someone had put on a record by a punk band calling themselves 'The Mass-Murderers'. A cacophonous dirge, Saul thought sourly. The atmosphere in the room seemed darker, as if the air had thickened with some indefinable menace. Lady Macbeth was dancing with a tall punk in black leathers, her bloody fingers twisting in his coarse spiked hair. Dracula was dancing with Little Dorrit.

'Annihilation is so fashionable,' said a voice in his ear. Someone handed him a joint.

It seemed to him there had been a deterioration in the general appearance of the other party-goers, a disintegration of identity. What had been sharp and clear was now blurred. Costumes were ripped and stained, masks discarded in the heat. Maybe character was no more than skin-deep, Saul thought. Or perhaps it was only at the point of dissolution that people's true identities emerged. He found a glass in his hand and finished what was in it. His reflection in the long mirror seemed distorted, elongated in its suit of sables, his face the cadaverous mask of a figure in an El Greco painting. An attendant lord.

From the kitchen came a confused noise of shouting, furniture being overturned and breaking glass.

'Watch out for emotional wreckage,' said Catherine, touching his arm.

'I will.' He knew it was no good asking her where she'd been, or with whom. 'Want to dance?'

The room seemed emptier than it had been before. Its inhabitants had no more substance than moonlit shadows. Dancing, it was easier to surrender to the pervasive unreality.

176

In the mirror their circling shapes were like figures glimpsed in a dream, familiar and unfamiliar in the same moment. The music stopped. There was no sound but the hiss and crackle of the silent record, endlessly revolving on its turntable.

12

Alone in the London Street apartment, Virginia sat on the edge of the bath in her unwieldy gown encrusted with costume jewellery. With one hand she gripped the rim of the basin, steadying herself; the other rested lightly on her abdomen. Taking soundings. Her eyes were closed, but against the reddish screen of blood-vessels was projected an image of dancing shapes – molecules or waltzing couples – the music accompanying their hectic revolutions the drumming of her own heart.

She winced as a spasm of something like pain, its ghostly simulacrum, passed through her. Pain but not pain. Slowly, her gaze fixed on the smeared white tiles of the sink unit, to which minute particles of blood and toothpaste adhered in patterns resembling those of the night sky, she began to count.

Certain things which had seemed impenetrable to her now made sense. She wondered how she could have failed to see what was clear to everyone but herself. A wilful blindness, undoubtedly. In her mind's eye she saw again the image of Saul dancing with the girl. His hands on her waist, his mouth against her hair. The other woman's figure – black swirling skirt, white neck, red mouth – was composed of a series of signs she had only just learned to read.

Virginia flinched, her eyes wide open. Pain. This time it was the real thing. She raised herself slowly. When she was standing she saw herself in the mirror over the basin. White scared face, wide eyes. To her surprise she saw that she was smiling, a smile of elation and terror. With extreme caution, she made her way into the hall to the telephone. As she dialled, failed to connect, misdialled, dialled again, she felt the pain begin. Pressing her hands flat against the wall for support, she breathed steadily, her body a conduit for sensation.

She held the receiver against her ear, its weight suddenly intolerable. Heard the connection, the ringing tone once, twice, three times before the call was answered. At once the silence was filled with the sound of voices, laughter, music, like the booming of distant waves in a conch shell.

'It's me,' she shouted. 'Virginia. Tell Saul I have to speak to him.'

But it became obvious after a while, during which she grew hoarse from shouting, that whoever had intercepted the call was no longer there. As she stood in the dark hall, vainly shouting her message into the void, the distant sound of revelry sounding to her ears like mocking laughter, she felt the next pain begin.

The implications of her abortive attempt to call for help only became apparent when she tried to call the hospital. She hung up, then picked up the phone to dial again. Instead of the dialling tone, however, there was the same confused sound she had heard before: voices shouting, the thump of a bass-line turned up too loud. Whoever had answered her call in the first place had left the receiver dangling, cutting her off from all other communication.

As the truth of this struck her she began to weep with frustration, pounding the futile mechanism until her knuckles were bruised. *Oh Jesus. Damn her. Stupid bitch. That stupid, smiling bitch.*

Calmer after her access of rage, she sucked her wounded fingers and considered her new-found knowledge. Suddenly, it all fell into place. Looks intercepted. Conversations overheard. Meaningless scraps, which taken together made a kind of sense. *Can't make it tonight.* It did not occur to her to blame Saul for what had happened. Towards her guilty husband she felt only a kind of pitying contempt.

The pains were more intense and – she guessed – closer

together. For a minute or two she fought a rising panic. What if it happened here, with no one around? She could bleed to death. Then, with an effort of will, she began to consider practicalities. Getting to a phone, for one. She started to put on her coat. In the dark she located her pocket book, then, in her eagerness, knocked it onto the floor. Keys, credit cards, change went flying into the darkness. Weeping, clenching her teeth against the pain, she got down on her hands and knees, her mind filled with atavistic images of women giving birth in this position, as she collected her scattered possessions.

As she struggled to pull herself upright, she heard the sound of a key in the lock. Her first thought was that Saul had got her message after all. The light went on.

'Goodness,' said Liz. 'Are you alright? Did you have a fall?'

'In a way,' she said, laughing now with mingled relief and disappointment.

'Where's Saul?' Guy helped her up, got her to a chair. 'Isn't he with you?'

'He stayed at Magda's.'

'Oh.' From the glance which passed between them, Virginia understood that her friends too had been party to duplicity.

'I'll make you a cup of tea,' Liz said.

'Maybe you'd better call me a taxi first,' said Virginia.

Virginia lay on her side in the high narrow hospital bed, on a plastic sheet that crackled with every movement. She slept fitfully, a drugged sleep, drowning in nightmares. An hour later she woke to intense pain. It was as if her flesh had dissolved, turned to a trembling, weeping jelly. She cried out. Immediately two women, in dark blue dresses with wide cummerbunds the colour of arterial blood, came to her. They raised her shuddering body, monitoring her pulse-rate, blood-pressure and the rate of her contractions, inserting cool, manicured fingers to check the precise dilation of her cervix.

They conferred in low voices. She heard the phrase *break the waters* and felt a premonitory shiver.

One of them bent over her. 'Your husband rang. He'll be with you in a wee while.'

'But that's impossible,' she said. 'My husband doesn't know. You see . . .'

'Hush now.' The nurse stroked Virginia's forehead while her companion prepared a syringe. 'Time for sleep.'

In a dream she watched the needle slide beneath the skin. Flecks of blood spotted the white hospital gown. *Like Snow White*, she thought, or perhaps said aloud, seeing the fleeting smile on the lips of the sandy-haired nurse. *Red as blood, white as snow, black as ebony*. Virginia slept.

She dreamed she was in a grey room, looking at a blank screen. From next door came the sound of a party in progress: laughter, the clinking of glasses. She could discern fragments of conversation, none of which made sense. She was unable to take her eyes from the flickering screen, across which dancing shapes were moving. If she watched long enough, everything would become clear . . .

When she woke again Saul was bending over her, saying her name. She was struck by how pale he was, his skin the colour of paper or dirty snow. It made her cold just looking at him. I'm so cold, she wanted to tell him, but her teeth were chattering so hard she couldn't speak. Why was it so cold?

'Listen,' he whispered – why was he whispering? – 'I'm sorry. I had no idea . . . Oh, God, I'm so sorry . . .' His eyes were full of tears.

'It's okay,' she said. A strange, weak voice that was not her own. 'It doesn't matter now.'

The dark nurse stood at the end of the bed. Virginia concentrated on the woman's face, seeing with extraordinary clarity her thin nose like the beak of some strange bird, her dark eyebrows, the faint down on her upper lip. She was explaining something, Virginia realized. Only it was hard to make it out . . .

'Your contractions seem to have stopped. We need to speed things up a little. Otherwise it could take hours . . .'

What was she saying? *Speed things up.* Through a haze of pain, Virginia watched as the dark nurse selected an instrument from the tray. An ivory wand.

'Just open your legs a wee bit. It won't take a second . . .' She saw Saul flinch and look away, as the wand was inserted, feeling herself part of some alien ritual. A blood sacrifice. The waters broke and leaked out of her.

'Lovely,' said the dark nurse, her task completed. 'Won't be long now.'

It was getting light outside the milky frosted glass window. The faces of the two women bending over her to examine her wracked body reflected her own exhaustion. She turned her head stiffly on the pillow to look at Saul, crouched miserably on a chair beside the bed, and was suddenly afraid. Did women still die in childbirth? She thought about it. Everything she had read on the subject had glossed over the possibility. Saul's eyelids were red. Traces of the make-up he had worn at the party adhered to his face, intensifying his pallor.

'Am I dying?' she said, hardly aware that she had spoken.

The sandy-haired nurse looked affronted. 'Och no,' she said. 'You'll no' die yet.'

The trolley ricocheted crazily along the corridor, propelled by an auxiliary whose face she never saw. When they reached the delivery room she was helped onto the table by two nurses, strangers to her. One propped her up with pillows so that she was nearly squatting. The other slid a long silver needle into her arm. When she looked down she could see the sliver of metal beneath the skin, connected by a plastic tube to the glucose drip above her head.

'Let's have a look at you.' One of the new nurses – the tall, thin one with the cold sore on her lip – bent over her. Moving Virginia's knees apart, she inserted two fingers, then three, into her patient's vagina. 'Ten centimetres. We're getting there.'

Getting where? Virginia wondered. Everyone seemed to know except her. She shifted her weight on the high metal bed, trying to find some relief from the dragging ache in her back, the tremor in her legs. But each change of position offered its own variation of pain.

Concluding her examination, the tall nurse raised the blood-spattered gown, exposing Virginia's swollen belly. She smeared a cold, colourless grease over its hard bulge, its bruise-coloured, distended navel. When this was done she strapped a metal disc to Virginia's abdomen, connecting it to a monitor. At once the flickering green light of the foetal heartbeat appeared on the screen and the twin pencils recording the rate of contractions began their manic scribble.

The other nurse, the small pretty one, turned to Saul. 'Would you care for a cup of tea?' she said.

Time had changed to a fluid medium, on which Virginia felt herself buoyed up, like a cork on the surface of a rapidly flowing stream, or a small craft about to be engulfed by a whirlpool. She had forgotten the purpose for which she was detained there, spreadeagled on the high bed in a web of plastic tubes and wires.

'Are we waiting for someone?' she said. The pretty nurse stifled a smile.

'Dr Glass has been delayed. An emergency. He'll be here as soon as he can.'

Virginia closed her eyes. It seemed to her there must be a way of separating herself from her body, that gross thing on the table which had betrayed her to pain and violation. If she could just cut loose. Break the connection. All it needed was an effort of will . . .

A commotion in the room beyond recalled her to herself. The rubber doors of the delivery room burst open and a man in green pyjamas and a skull-cap came in, shouting instructions.

'Let's get moving. Get us a cup of tea, nurse, I'm parched. God, the last one was a bugger. Haemorrhage. Thought I'd never get away.'

He washed and dried his hands. When he had positioned Virginia to his satisfaction he sat down beside the bed and began to insert a long needle into her spinal nerve, muttering encouragement to himself under his breath. 'Come on, come on, come *on*. Christ, I could do with a cigarette.'

'I put two sugars in.' The pretty nurse returned with two cups of tea, one of which she handed to Saul, who stared at the cup in his hand as if amazed. His gaze shifted with appalled fascination to the anaesthetist's needlework.

'Good girl.' Dr Glass smacked his lips appreciatively as he probed and fiddled. 'Just the way I like it. Hot and sweet.'

'I think I'll go outside for a minute,' said Saul.

'It gets them every time,' the anaesthetist said in Virginia's ear. 'As soon as they see the old needle go in . . .'

'I'm glad I can't see it,' she said.

'You get used to it once you've done a couple of hundred. Okey-dokey, lovey, that should do the trick for now.'

As the drug hit Virginia's bloodstream it was as if a switch had been thrown. The pain vanished and everything sparkled with unnatural radiance. When she looked down she could see her hands, greenish as a reptile's skin in the glassy light, and her legs, very thin and white, sticking out on either side of her straining belly.

'How do you feel?' Saul returned, his face blanched with fatigue. She felt a rush of sympathy for him, with his hangdog look, his guilty secrets. He met her eyes.

'Oh, terrific,' she said, attempting a smile. 'Just terrific.'

The contractions grew stronger. The nurses took up their stations on either side of the bed, bracing Virginia's feet against their red waistbands, so that she was leaning her weight against them, her body half-crouching.

'Come on, push.'

'You can do it . . .'

'*Push.*'

With every thrust she had the sensation she was about to turn inside out, spilling her body's contents – guts liver heart lungs kidneys – onto the table.

The contraction passed and she rested, closing her eyes for what might have been seconds or hours, before the next one rose like a wave about to break. On the monitor screen the green light pulsed, the scribbling pencils described mountain ranges, Gothic spires.

'Here comes another one . . .'

'*Push.*'

But all her effort was in vain. The child was spinning in the womb, each push only serving to thrust it further back into the confined space from which it struggled to break.

'You're nearly there. Feel . . .' The midwife took Virginia's hand and placed it so that she could feel the child's head. The texture was hard, slippery, unmistakably Other. She shuddered and withdrew her questing fingers, with a vision of that blind, desperate struggle to be born into mess and horror.

'Get ready for the next one . . .'

'*Push.*'

Her throat hurt with effort, she had no strength left. She braced herself against the scarlet waistbands as the wave swelled, curled and broke, knocking the breath from her body.

'Some indication of foetal distress . . .'

Something was happening to the green light on the monitor, which had pulsed with a steady rhythm hour after hour. A break in the pattern, a random fluttering. The tall nurse went to the wall-phone and spoke into it.

A few minutes passed and doors flapped open. A bald man in a white coat rushed in, checking his watch. 'How long has it been going on?' he demanded angrily. The nurse murmured something, too softly for Virginia to hear. 'Too long, too long,' he said, cutting short the explanation. 'You'll have to cut her.'

Suddenly the room was full of people. Doctors in masks and gowns. Nurses with silver dishes of instruments. Content with her spectator's role, Virginia watched as her legs were hoisted into stirrups on either side of the bed. The bald man reappeared, wearing a green gown, his face half hidden behind a surgical mask. She saw the pretty nurse hand him what looked like a pair of scissors. She felt Saul take her hand.

The sound of her vagina being snipped open was exactly that of cloth being cut. When the forceps entered her it was a sensation like walking into the edge of a table. Breathing shallowly, as instructed, she watched as the surgeon extracted her child's head, fragile as an egg between two spoons. She was unprepared for the muscular slither, like that of a landed fish, as her son was pulled out and slapped on her stomach, wet with blood. His open eyes blue-black, fathomless as space.

When he left her, Virginia was asleep. The child was beside her, in the plastic cot that reminded Saul of a fishtank. His son slept with ferocious concentration, his red fists clenched, as if exhausted by his first hour of independence. In the corridor Saul almost collided with an empty trolley wheeled by an orderly, who shouted after him good-humouredly. In the lift, two off-duty nurses smiled at him. He bought a cup of coffee from the hot-drinks dispenser in the waiting room. Seeing himself reflected in its chrome surfaces – his face unshaven, his eyes red from sleeplessness – he realized why they had smiled. He was conspicuous, a figure of comedy. The new father.

Outside it was starting to get light. He turned without reflection towards the Meadows. In his present state, sleep was impossible. His mind was racing, his pulse trembled with elation. It had not occurred to him he would have a son. Through the long months, the fitful tedium of Virginia's pregnancy, he had – deliberately, it seemed to him now – failed to consider the idea at all. It was as if they had no connection, the fact of pregnancy and the fact of childbirth. Even now he found it hard to connect the two.

He reached the borders of the park. There was no one around. He had never felt so alone, so aware of his uniqueness. It was if he were the only one left alive in a blasted landscape. He crossed the wide expanse of grass, still wet with dew. In front of him rose a dark mass of rock; the foothills of the volcano. The path rose in a shallow curve, becoming steeper after a while. He began to climb.

At the first bend in the path, he rested, leaning against the sheer wall of rock, his gaze moving across the dark horizon. In his mind's eye he saw Virginia's face as he had seen it some hours before. The pupils of the eyes dilated. The mouth a parched hole, gasping for air. He felt as if he had never really seen her until that moment, as if what he had seen was the real face, beneath the composed mask. 'I'm sorry,' he had said to her, uncertain even as he said it what it was he meant. Was it an apology for letting her down, for not being there when she needed him, or was he admitting culpability for some more serious misdemeanour? 'It's okay,' she had said. 'It doesn't matter now.' She had forgiven him his transgression it seemed. Only he was not sure which one.

He had arrived back at the apartment with Catherine around two, to find Liz waiting up for him. It was clear from her tone as she told him what had happened that she did not think well of him. He'd had to change out of his costume, ripping off buttons and tearing seams in his haste. Catherine had watched him dress. When he was ready to leave, she came with him to the door, still in her party clothes.

'I'm sorry it had to happen like this.'

'It's not your fault.' Although, even as he'd said it, he found himself starting to blame her a little.

He slipped on a piece of loose rock and almost fell, glancing round involuntarily, as if someone might have witnessed his momentary loss of equilibrium. He was on the edge. Below him, a lip of bare rock, then a steep plunge into the void. It would be so easy, he thought, with a sudden burst of hilarity, to bring the whole mess to an end. All he had to do was lean over, further, a little further, until the tenuous relationship he had with the earth was lost. He would hardly need to exert himself at all. It would be enough just to surrender . . . He brought himself back from the thought with a nervous shudder. It was hysteria, he thought, induced by emotional strain. Morbid imagination.

At the summit of the crag he paused to catch his breath. Above him lay the volcano, its broken cone a black shape against the sky, in which a few stars still glimmered. Four hundred feet below lay the city. In the grey light it seemed a city of ash, of drifting smoke. Gazing from his mountain top, he had the feeling he was looking at the past. His thoughts returned to Catherine. There had always been something a shade immature about the relationship, he felt. His love for her – if it was love – seemed like a dream from which he had just awakened. All that was over now.

He took off his jacket and folded it into a rough pillow in the curve of the rock. Then he sat down with his back to the mountain, realizing with a vague shock of annoyance that he was out of cigarettes. He closed his eyes, slept for a few minutes.

Along the horizon the sky turned from pale green to pink. As he watched, the red sun popped between two hills, like a child's head from the birth canal. A warm light touched spires, domes, rooftops, so that it no longer seemed a city of the dead, but a celestial vision. City of God, he thought, his breath clouding the cold air. He felt a surge of exhilaration that was the obverse of his earlier hysteria. It was good, after all, to be alive. His eye followed the trajectory of a bird, a thousand feet above him in the aether. From where he stood he could see the hospital buildings, half hidden by trees. His wife and son slept on while he kept his vigil, as if that alone could shield them from harm.

Catherine's decision, taken in the early hours of the morning, to tell Virginia everything about her affair with Saul vanished the minute she walked into the room where the other woman was lying, apparently asleep, on the high hospital bed. From where she stood in the doorway it was impossible to tell whether Virginia's eyes were open or closed. All she could see was the dark tangle of her hair on the pillow and, above the stiff sheet, her arm, its thin wrist encircled by a plastic bracelet bearing her name. She took a faltering step or two towards the bed, uncertain whether to go or stay. Her gift of white chrysanthemums sat awkwardly in the crook of her arm.

Virginia stirred. 'Why, Cathy, what a nice surprise.' She struggled to sit upright. 'Come on over. God, I can't tell you how good it is to see you. I've been going crazy in here. Nothing to do but sleep and eat.'

'I brought you some flowers.' Even before Virginia had spoken, she had resolved to say nothing. The idea was lunacy, the product of an over-stimulated imagination. What had possessed her to consider it? She felt as relieved as if she had stepped back from the edge of a frightful drop. 'White was all I could find. A bit funereal, I'm afraid, but . . .'

'They're lovely. What a sweet thought.' Virginia, as Catherine might have foreseen, was more in control of the situation than she was. She sat, perfectly composed, arranging the lace sleeves of her gown to cover the bruises left by the IV needle.

'How are you?' Catherine said, still appalled by her own temerity. (Christ! She'd even rehearsed the things she meant to say: 'Virginia, there's something I think you ought to know . . .'; 'Virginia, Saul and I . . .') 'You look wonderful.'

'I feel fat. Nobody told me I'd still have the bump after the baby came out. They give you weird stuff to eat in here. Porridge, macaroni cheese . . .'

'It must be nourishing. And cheap, I suppose.'

'It tastes awful. Hey, do you have a lipstick I can borrow? When Saul packed my case he forgot to put any make-up in. Typical man.'

It seemed to Catherine there was a diffidence about the way Virginia said her husband's name. I'm imagining things, she thought. And looked up to find Virginia's gaze upon her.

'You don't mind, do you?' she said. 'Only some people hate lending intimate possessions . . .'

'I don't mind. Here . . .' Catherine rummaged in her bag for compact, lipstick, eyeliner. 'Keep them,' she said.

'Its okay, it's only till Saul brings the rest of my stuff.'

Again, there seemed a slight hesitation as she pronounced his name. As if testing its effect. Perhaps she wants me to leave so she can be alone with him, thought Catherine, relieved to have hit upon so innocuous an explanation. 'I ought to be going,' she said. 'I only looked in for a minute.'

'You can't go yet.' Her disappointment seemed unfeigned, however. 'You haven't seen the baby. They'll be bringing him for his four o'clock feed any second. You'll wait, won't you? He's the cutest thing. The image of his daddy.'

'Of course I'll wait. If you're sure I won't be in the way.'

'What makes you think that?' Virginia snapped open the compact and began to powder her nose. Then she applied a coat of Catherine's dark red lipstick. 'Not really my shade, is it?' she said, pursing her lips as if for a kiss.

It was hard to see even the barest resemblance between her lover's physiognomy and that of the baby. They seemed, in fact, to belong to different species. With its wrinkled face and long thin fingers, the child resembled some intelligent, night-dwelling creature. A marmoset, thought Catherine, feeling the prehensile strength in the tiny hands.

'Hold him for me a minute, will you?' Virginia made some

adjustment to the arrangement of flaps and fastenings at the front of her nightdress. 'These nurses never give you time to get ready, they just dump the kid and run.'

Catherine held the little body, swaddled in its blanket, in the crook of her arm. The big head lolled on its weak stalk, snapped forward against her breast. She touched the dark-haired, surprisingly hot skull, feeling the pulsing triangle at its centre. Eyes black as chips of onyx winked at her, then vanished between bruised lids. The miniature nose wrinkled and a thin cry issued from the gaping mouth.

'Will you listen to that,' said Virginia, holding out her arms. 'Such a little *man*.' She tucked the baby comfortably under her large, exposed breast and guided the nipple into his mouth. At once his colour changed from red to pale, his taut body relaxed, his eyes closed.

'What are you going to call him?'

'We thought maybe Aaron John. John after my father. But I don't know. Maybe we'll wait a few days and see if he still looks like an Aaron or not . . .'

'Sure he looks like an Aaron.' Saul stood in the doorway, holding a large, tissue-paper wrapped bunch of pale blue carnations.

'Hi darling.' Virginia lifted her face to be kissed. 'Look who else dropped in.'

'I've been admiring your son,' said Catherine.

'Hi.' Saul's smile involved the minimum of facial muscles. Above it, his eyes were apprehensive, as if she were the thirteenth fairy at the christening. 'He's pretty special, isn't he?' he said.

'He's beautiful.' Catherine stood up. 'I was just leaving . . .'

'Stay a little while,' said Virginia. 'Saul darling, why don't you see if you can get Cathy a cup of coffee?'

When the echo of his footsteps had died away down the corridor she looked at Catherine. 'I think you ought to know I'm not about to give him up,' she said with a faint smile.

Returning the smile before she caught the sense of the words, Catherine felt her heart jump. Her smile faltered. 'What do you mean?' It was suddenly an effort to hold the other's gaze. To look away, she felt, would signify defeat. An admission of guilt.

'Oh, come on,' said Virginia. 'You know what I'm talking about. You had an affair with my husband. Maybe it's still going on . . .'

'No.'

'Well, that's something, I guess. Because it can't go on.' She stroked the small dark head of the sleeping infant at her breast. 'The fact is, Saul has commitments now.'

'How long have you known?'

'Not very long. Since the night of the party. Although I sort of knew something was going on a while back.' She hesitated. 'I found a letter. A note. It wasn't much in itself, but . . .'

'Enough to be going on with,' said Catherine. Despite the temperature of the ward, she felt herself shiver as if at the onset of flu.

'That's right.' Virginia shifted the child from one arm to the other. Startled, it gave an indignant cry. 'Hush, now,' she murmured. She looked at Catherine for a minute or two. A meditative look. 'It sounds stupid, but – I really liked you, you know? I guess it shows how wrong you can be about somebody.'

Saul returned with the coffee. 'How's my son today?' he said.

'Hungry as ever. He just can't get enough.' Virginia took a sip of coffee and made a face. 'Oh darling, you forgot the sugar.'

'That stupid machine. I'll get you another,' said Saul.

'One thing I want to know,' Virginia said, when they were alone, 'is when did it start?'

'Some time ago.'

'Before or after I arrived?'

'Before.'

Virginia was silent a moment. 'I don't know if that makes me feel better or worse,' she said.

'I'm sorry . . .'

Virginia shrugged, as if contrition, coming this late in the day, were beside the point. Which it was, Catherine thought.

'One other thing. Saul doesn't know. That I know, I mean.'

'He won't hear it from me. If that's what's worrying you.'

'Oh, I'm not worried about a thing,' Virginia said with a small, pained smile.

Saul returned. The three of them sat for a few minutes, discussing inconsequential things. Blue carnations. The weather. Institutional food. The child, sated with milk, fell asleep. Saul went to find the nurse. Catherine took her leave. At the door she glanced back. Her last image of them, almost. Holy Family with attendant saint. A triptych. The departing penitent in the third panel giving the composition its centripetal force.

13

Catherine waited for Saul in the Circle Bar at the Café Royale. It was the night before Virginia was due to come home; it was raining, he was late. She clicked her nails on the rim of the empty glass, thinking about things he'd said. Above her head twin pillars shaped like gilded palm trees with enormous curving leaves supported the ornate ceiling, their image multiplied in arched mirrors, which in turn reflected the shape of the windows giving onto the street.

'Hi. Sorry I'm late. I couldn't get away. She's so excited about going home.'

'When do you leave?'

'Oh, not for a few days. I . . . Let me buy you a drink first.' He seemed nervous, evasive. When he returned with the drinks they sat for a few minutes transfixed by shyness. 'Hey,' he said, 'you had your hair cut. It suits you. Really.'

'Thanks.' She reached over and brushed a strand of hair from his face. 'Yours is all wet.'

'It's raining.' The brief contact seemed to break the tension between them. 'I had a letter from Cornell a couple of days ago,' Saul said. 'They've agreed to let me finish my PhD there next year, taking the year I've done here into account. Apparently there's a guy in the English department who's a friend of Richardson's. Thinks he's the greatest thing since sliced bread. Richardson's written me this really nice reference . . .'

'Good for Richardson. When do you start?'

'January third. Virginia's going to stay with her parents for a week or two while I look for somewhere to live . . .' He was silent for a minute. 'Look, I'm sorry,' he said, not meeting her gaze.

'Don't be. It's good news. Cornell was your first choice, wasn't it?'

'Yes, but . . .'

'It wouldn't have worked here. Not with the baby. And Virginia wasn't happy.'

'I guess you're right,' he said after a pause. 'It wouldn't have worked.'

'Another drink?' she said. 'We might as well make a night of it.'

'Sure, why not?' He touched her hand. Seemed about to say something, checked himself, then said it anyway. 'I can't tell you how much I appreciate it. I mean, your attitude. I thought . . . Oh, this sounds stupid, I know, but . . .'

'You thought I might give you a hard time.'

'Something like that.' He grinned with relief. 'I should have known you'd be reasonable about the whole thing.'

'Try me in a couple of hours, after I've had a few drinks.' Catherine took the empty glass out of his hand. 'I might not be so bloody reasonable then . . .'

The first flicker of lightning appeared above the distant line of hills. In the dark the flashes were violet, leaving an after-image of black. The sound of thunder came as a relief. Later came the rain.

They sat and watched it for an hour in the high-ceilinged room with its tarnished gilt lamps, its painted palm trees. Around them, people were speaking in low voices, the sound lost in the vaulted space. There was a smell of spilled beer and smoke. From the street came the wet swish of passing cars. As they sat, becalmed, Catherine had a vision of eternity as a place not unlike this, where you waited at a smeared and cigarette-burned table covered with empty glasses, in the draught from ill-fitting swing doors, for someone to begin speaking. I'm drunk, she thought.

'Let's go,' said Saul. He put his arm around her as they went out into the raining dark.

*

Liz was in the kitchen making tea when they came in, their hair and clothes soaked.

'It's a wet night for walking,' she said, giving them a quizzical look.

'Oh, we like it,' said Saul. 'It suits our mood of perversity.' Water ran down his face from the ends of his wet hair. 'God I'll miss this place,' he said, peeling off his jacket. 'It's so elemental.'

'We'll make a Scotsman of you yet,' said Liz, scalding the pot.

'Saul's going to be leaving us soon.' Catherine's voice was muffled by the towel with which she was drying her hair. 'He and Virginia and the baby are going back to the States next week.'

'Well,' said Liz, 'we'll be sorry to lose you.'

'I'm sorry to be leaving,' said Saul.

In the sitting room Guy was sitting in front of the fire, doing the *Guardian* crossword. Liz poured out tea. In the firelight her brown skin and hair had the patina of bronze, like a carved image of some goddess of the hearth.

'Guy and I have some news of our own,' she said.

'Liz is pregnant.' Guy's round blue eyes beamed under his boyish fringe. 'We've only just heard.'

'That's wonderful,' Saul said. With the absurd formality men reserve for such occasions, he and Guy shook hands.

'It seems like a night for celebrations.' Catherine poured out four measures of whisky and handed them round. 'I think this calls for a toast.'

Liz waved the glass away. 'I'll stick to tea,' she said. 'What are we drinking to, anyway? The king over the water?'

'To love,' said Saul, looking at Catherine. It was a night for sentimental gestures.

'Annihilation,' she said. 'What else?'

'Oh, I'm not having that,' Liz said firmly. 'Where I come from we do things properly, or not at all. To the future.' She raised her cracked teacup. 'Whatever it may bring.'

'It comes to the same thing,' said Catherine. It occurred to her she was taking it very well. All around her domestic circles were closing. Her friends were succumbing to biological imperative. The triumph of DNA. It sounded like the title of an eighteenth-century genre painting. Madonna and child, with household gods.

Liz and Guy went to bed. Saul switched off the lamp and they sat for a while, drowsy with heat, in the firelight. Saul rested his head on Catherine's shoulder.

'I'm going to miss you,' he said. She did not reply. Reading her silence as indifference, he gave way to self-pity. 'I can't tell you how hard this is for me . . .'

'Then don't.' Her tone was unexpectedly sharp. 'You know you don't mean it.'

'Don't say that. If you knew how I felt about you . . .'

'All you think about is your own feelings. And hers.'

'That's not true . . .'

'Isn't it?'

'No . . .'

'You're going back with her, aren't you?' Her voice shook. He saw that she was crying.

'Catherine . . .' He took her in his arms. 'Oh, baby . . .'

She felt herself beginning to sink, like a swimmer in difficulties coming up for the last time, and a small cold voice in the back of her head said: *This is it. You might as well say it.*

'I love you,' she said, surrendering herself to the treacherous current, and he, with the relief of one who has, more by luck than judgement, escaped drowning, murmured, 'Let's go to bed.'

In the morning Catherine sat at the big pine table in the kitchen while Saul settled his accounts with Liz. Last night had also been a settling of accounts, she thought.

'Then there's just the matter of the electricity bill,' Liz was saying, running her hands distractedly through her hair. Her face had the greasy pallor of early pregnancy. She was eating dry toast and drinking black tea.

'Let's split it,' said Saul, waving aside her muted protests.

'Well, if you insist . . .' Liz gave a wan smile. 'I'm not in the mood for an argument.' She pushed aside her cup with a grimace of disgust. 'I feel terrible. The mornings are the worst.' She glanced shyly at Saul. 'As you know.'

'When I think of what Virginia went through,' he said, 'it makes me wonder how you women stand it.'

'We don't have an awful lot of choice,' Liz said drily. 'Is it tonight you're bringing her home from the hospital?'

'If that's okay. It's only for a few days.'

'It'll be nice to have a baby in the house,' said Liz. 'Practice for me and Guy.' She glanced at her watch. 'I must go. Or the little beasts will be tearing the place apart.'

The heavy street door shut behind her.

'I'll make some coffee,' said Catherine. The sound of the struck match was enormous in the quiet room. She filled the kettle and set it on the circle of blue flames, then sat down opposite him. For a few minutes neither spoke, both fixed in their absurd tableau of regret. Saul did not look at her, cradling his head in his hands.

'I guess you think I've acted like a complete bastard, right?'

'Why should I think that?' She measured spoonfuls of coffee into the jug.

'Last night . . . I never intended . . . Oh God this sounds so stupid. I just wanted to *talk* to you, you know? Settle it, like adults.'

'Things never turn out quite the way you expect, do they?'

'I had it all worked out. The research place at Cornell. Virginia and me. The baby. It all seemed to fit.' He looked at her. 'Only now I'm not so sure . . .'

'What do you mean?' Her gaze was fixed on the wavering jet of steam issuing from the kettle's spout. In a few seconds, she judged, its shriek would disturb the quiet. She grew tense with the expectation.

'I seem to have gotten involved again,' said Saul, a touch resentfully.

'Oh, I don't think so,' she said. 'Last night wasn't important.'

'But you said . . .'

'You don't think for one moment I was serious, do you?' Catherine reached to silence the breathless scream of the kettle. She poured a jet of boiling water onto the dark grounds, watching them froth and rise. 'Think of it as evening the score.'

Watching him out of the corner of her eye as they sat awaiting take-off in the cushioned cell of the aeroplane, Virginia saw that her husband's thoughts were elsewhere. It didn't take much imagination to work out where, or with whom. Although seeing him and Catherine together in those last few days it had been hard to believe there had ever been anything between them. They'd been as distant as strangers, Virginia thought. If she hadn't had confirmation of the affair from Catherine's own lips, she'd have been inclined to think she had imagined the whole thing.

Once or twice since that conversation with Catherine, she'd thought about confronting her husband with what she knew, but the impulse weakened with each successive day. She saw now that it would be knowledge she kept in reserve, for use on some future occasion, if such an occasion arose. As things were, there seemed little point in jeopardizing the situation. If Saul chose to believe she knew nothing, she was in no hurry to disillusion him. For once in her life, Virginia thought, looking down at the sleeping child in her arms, she held all the cards.

Saul stared out at the stretch of grey tarmac and the grey buildings beyond, all that was visible of the world through the window of the wheeling plane. He was not, in fact, thinking about Catherine at all. The events of the past few days had set a kind of seal on what had taken place between them, so that, if he thought of it at all, it was as something which had happened a long time ago, to someone else perhaps. He'd think about it sometime, he knew, but not right now.

His mind focused, instead, on a memory of himself as he'd been a year ago, disembarking at Heathrow after the first stage of his journey north. A serious young man in a new raincoat, filled with anticipation for what was before him. How naive he'd been, he thought, how trusting. Considering himself as he had been then, only a few short months before, it was hard to believe he was the same person. Something – the experience of fatherhood perhaps, or merely a growing awareness of his capacity for dissimulation – had changed him forever. His life seemed, somehow, infinitely richer in complexities – in possibilities – than it had been before. The plane taxied along the runway, gathered speed and took off, with that familiar vertiginous sensation of release. At the moment of losing contact with the ground, Saul felt himself divested of his earlier, immature self; new selves, new lives awaited him, to make of them what he would. It was only then, relinquishing the past, that he thought of Catherine. He turned from the window. London, swathed in grey sheets of rain, fell away beneath.

His gaze, too long distracted, focused at last on Virginia. She met his eyes, unsmilingly. A long, steady look – perhaps of understanding – passed between them. Saul took her hand and they sat for a while without speaking, watching the face of their sleeping child, secure in his carrycot on the seat between them. From time to time a dream shivered across his features, but he did not wake.

It was only when the affair was over, in the weeks following the Meyers' departure, that Catherine realized how completely she had misjudged the situation. In the complex relations between married people she had played a minor and ultimately dispensable role. Feeling herself to be a disruptive element, she had in fact been an agent of reconciliation. The irony of it was not one she could enjoy.

She had the feeling of having been jettisoned, a cast-off costume or an unwanted prop in a play which had finished its season. Her character (a minor role, after all) had been given to someone else or perhaps written out of the script altogether. Now she lounged, cooling her heels, while around her the real business of living went on. Birth, copulation and death. She felt at a distance from it all.

In those last weeks of term she found her concentration gone. Sometimes, sitting at her desk in the library, she returned to consciousness with a start, aware that she had been staring at the same page for a long time, finding herself unable to recall a line of what she had been reading. The days had a flatness like that of a coarse-grained photograph, all subtle gradations of tone eliminated. Nothing but dead black, empty white.

Nights were the worst. She wasn't sleeping well at all. All night long there was the sound of insane laughter, shouting in the street. Car doors slamming, loud music. At five the early morning traffic began. Night workers returning home. The soft rattle of milk-floats. Around this time her fellow insomniac in the flat downstairs began his saxophone practice. She listened to the high, cool notes and shivered in her damp sheets.

Saul was a ghost in her bed. When she turned over, restless in the dark, it was to clasp the outline of his shape beside her, to feel on the pillow next to hers the imprint of his head. His leaving was as absolute as death. It was as if she or some part of her had died. Perhaps a better analogy was that of amputation. She felt as if she had lost a limb – an arm or a leg, say – some useful but not essential part. It was this she could still feel, a ghostly presence, a reminder of her undivided state.

It struck her that an act of exorcism was called for.

*

Catherine went to a party. It was a month since Saul had left. A night in early November. She stopped off for some cigarettes at a pub in Broughton Street she'd often passed but never entered. The interior was dark red. Thick glass panes permitted the minimum amount of light into a room resembling a tunnel or a hole in the rock. She was conscious of a silence as she walked up to the bar. For some reason she couldn't afterwards fathom, she decided to stay for a drink.

Several drinks later, she accepted a lift to a party in Craigmillar from a boy called Davis or Davie and his two friends. She sat next to Davis or Davie who was driving. The two friends sat in the back. From time to time during the course of the drive, which took longer than she'd expected, one muttered something to the other and there was a burst of laughter. She had the uneasy feeling that the butt of this particular joke was herself.

Craigmillar was a drab ghetto of postwar council houses, steel-shuttered off-licences and concrete bus shelters decorated with obscene drawings. Between the gable-ends of houses were strips of wasteground covered with rubbish. Burnt-out hulks of cars, ripped mattresses, trashed settees. As they cruised the maze of streets in search of the party the darkness was pierced by the chemical flares of rockets and roman candles. Shadowy figures backlit by flames were visible for an instant, then lost. The acrid smoke of recent detonations hung in the streets.

At last the car pulled up in front of a small, mean house, at the end of a terrace of identical houses rendered in crumbling grey concrete. Inside, her eyes took a few minutes to adjust to the darkness. By the imperfect light of the red bulb in the front room she could make out shapes of bodies slumped on the floor. From a room at the back came music, of a kind. A scratchy whining, overlaid with static.

Davis, who seemed to know his way, went into the kitchen, returning empty handed. The beer had run out. He produced a bottle of vodka from inside his jacket, took a drink and handed it to her. 'Dance?' he said.

There was a radio playing in the room. Davis and Catherine were the only ones dancing. Between tracks he passed her the bottle. Warm vodka ran down her chin as she drank. In the red light they kept up a shuffling, circling momentum, as if only this kept them from falling. She put her head on his shoulder.

'She's a pro,' muttered Davis in her ear.

'What?'

'I said, she's a pro.' He indicated a small blonde with a wizened face. She might have been fifty or twenty, it was hard to tell in that light.

'So's that one . . . and that one . . .' he breathed, as they jigged and turned. 'Whores,' he murmured, tenderly as a caress.

Several other couples got up to dance. In such a small space collision seemed inevitable, Catherine thought, with a dull sense of being no longer in control of her actions. Miraculously, it seemed, they avoided making contact with the other dancers, each pair circling within its allotted zone. Maybe it was just that Davis wasn't as drunk as she was. The music changed. A demonic howling filled the room. Davis was shouting something; he had to repeat it several times before she understood.

'I said, are you married?'

'No,' she said. 'I'm not.' She began to laugh.

'It's all right,' Davis said, patting her back as she sobbed and hiccoughed, 'there's no need to take on.' The vodka was almost finished. He handed her the bottle. 'Have another drink,' he said.

Later they went upstairs. They found an empty room and she lay on the bed while Davis removed her shoes and tights. He didn't waste time on preliminaries. As they fucked she had to bite her lips to stop herself from laughing aloud.

*

When she came to, grey light was filtering through half-drawn curtains onto the wrecked bed. Her memories of what had happened the night before were confused. She sat up and saw she was not alone. On the bed next to her one of Davis's friends, the ugly one, was sleeping. Someone else was asleep on the floor under a tangle of blankets. Of Davis himself there was no sign. She swung her legs out of bed and felt around for her shoes. She had the crazy thought everything would be all right, if she could just find her shoes.

She got up. Her companion on the bed groaned and stirred in his sleep but did not wake. She was conscious of an urgent need to piss and of a violent thirst. In the cramped fetid bathroom down the hall, in which the peeling wallpaper had a pattern of tropical fish, she relieved the most pressing of these concerns. Her face in the mirror, a blunt, dry-eyed mask, appalled her. There were black rings of mascara around her eyes and a bite on her neck.

She reached down to put the plug in the basin, which was stained brown in a long scar from a tap that dripped, and her fingers encountered a smooth clot of human hair. She deposited it, strange relic, on the rim of a soap dish and ran some water into the sink. Slowly the mirror clouded with steam. Clumsily, as though she had forgotten the use of her hands, she slopped the blood-heat liquid over her cheeks, eyelids, nose and mouth.

Downstairs in the kitchen amongst still-life arrangements of crushed beer cans and overflowing ashtrays Catherine drank a glass of water. In the bleached light that fell through dirty panes the room and everything in it was the colour of ashes. She experienced a moment of stupid revelation. This is it, she thought, with a kind of dull relief. This is all there is. Leaning on the edge of the sink, the cold filthy floor beneath her bare feet, she laughed until the tears ran down her face.

The leaves in the Botanical Gardens were black with frost. Shivering and lifeless, they clung still to the trees. The flowers were all dead, except for some late roses rotting on the stem and the brittle clumps of heather rustling drily in the wind which swept the rain-streaked cliffs of the rock garden. *Blasted with sighs, surrounded with tears*.

The grass was damp with the last night's rain as she found the spot and sat down. Above her head rain dripped from wet shrubs or slid with a sudden sound from the shiny leaves of an evergreen. Here it was possible to sit entirely surrounded by leaves. A living room, thought Catherine, not a room for living. It occurred to her that if you broke off a twig or snapped a branch it might begin to bleed, like the trees in the Wood of Suicides. The macabre appositeness of the thought made her smile. In the summer she and Saul had made love here. She wondered if the flattened grass preserved somewhere in the deep patterning of its cells the memory of their entwined, warm-blooded bodies. A snapshot of disturbance.

The thought was not comforting. After a while, chilled to the bone, she got up and made for the hothouses. Walking between giant cacti in the artificial desert air she thought about death, about Saul and about the peripheral nature of her existence. Soon she began to feel better. There was consolation in despair. It was time to come to terms with what was past, since she could not obliterate it. Time to jettison emotional baggage.

It seemed to her that she had behaved rather well. She had made no demands, extracted no promises. If there was anything to be salvaged it was this. She thought of the last time she had seen Saul, getting into the cab which was taking them to the airport. She had watched from the window as he helped Virginia into the car, settling her into her seat, with the shawled infant on her lap, before walking round to the other side. He had opened the door, glancing up at the window where she stood. She saw in her mind's eye the pale oval of his face against the upturned collar of his dark coat. She had stepped away from the window. There had been the slam of a car door and the dull roar as the cab pulled away from the kerb. When she looked out again the street was empty.

Well, he was gone. She had lost the game. In the end all she had to sustain her was her intact pride. It wasn't much. Who else knew or cared how well she had behaved, apart from herself? And perhaps, after all, it had not been pride but cowardice which had been the deciding factor. Her reluctance to get involved. And for all his talk of commitment, Saul had behaved no better. Throughout it all, he had been skulking on the edge of the arena, trying to see which way the contest was going before pledging allegiance to either side. In time, she saw, the minor disturbance of his infidelity would be eclipsed by the greater shocks and rearrangements of parenthood. Work would absorb time he had devoted to love. For him, life had become a serious business.

As for herself, she had been nothing but a spectator at the Roman games of matrimony. She had not been thrown to the lions, it was true, but neither had she emerged with the spoils of victory. *Amor vincit omnia*, she thought sourly.

It was warm under the hothouse canopy. The winter sun filtered through its curved glass vault onto her upturned face. She closed her eyes. Around her the delicate flowers of cacti, pink as the flesh of the inner lip, bloomed in the unchanging air.

The decade was not yet over, but already there was a feeling things had been played out. It was the end of an era apparently. The end of the postwar boom. The end of the sexual revolution. Everything seemed tainted with a sepia wash of nostalgia. Or maybe it was just the reflection of her own jaundiced mood, Catherine thought.

'You should get out, while you still have the chance,' Jonathan said to her one day. They were having lunch in his rooms. He had lit a fire against the late November chill and the room had a faint, pleasant scent of burning pine. 'There's no future in academia anymore. The writing's on the wall.'

'Is that what you're going to do?' she asked, surprised. She had taken it for granted that Jonathan, like most of their friends, intended to pursue a career as a university lecturer.

He shrugged disdainfully. 'As soon as I can.' He cut a slice of bread and passed it to her. 'Well, can you see me teaching in some dreary polytechnic? God forbid.'

'What will you do?'

'Oh, you know, whatever transpires. Try some of this cheese, I think you'll like it. A friend of mine's offered me a partnership in a wine-importing business he's setting up. Of course, it would mean spending a lot of time in France . . .'

'I can see that might be hard for you,' Catherine said wryly. She considered her own options with a renewed sense of dissatisfaction. At the age of twenty-four her only experience had been academic. She had never worked. She couldn't even type. There seemed no alternative but to continue with what she was doing in the hope of gaining some kind of temporary appointment – research fellowship or junior lectureship – at the end of it. Although after the interview she had had with her supervisor a few days before, even that seemed in doubt. Hobson had been less than enthusiastic about her first draft, had hinted her approach lacked definition. There were those amongst his colleagues, he'd intimated, who'd been unhappy with the structuralist method she'd adopted; felt that radical redrafting was necessary. 'My advice, for what it's worth,' he'd said, concluding his remarks, 'is stay well clear of all this structuralist nonsense. Stick to literary criticism and you won't go far wrong . . .'

Perhaps misinterpreting her mood of dejection, Jonathan began to describe the break-up of his relationship with Sean, a student actor he'd met at a backstage party after a Fringe performance. For two weeks in August, they'd been everything to one another. But then Sean had returned to Bristol, to pursue his studies.

'And since then, not so much as a postcard,' Jonathan said. 'More wine?'

208

'I think Saul might have written to me. Although I can understand why he hasn't.'

'That was always your trouble.' He filled her glass. 'You were too understanding. Too reasonable about the whole thing. Maybe you should have tried being unreasonable. Men expect that from women.'

'Maybe.' She tried to picture Saul sitting down to write to her. How did one begin such a letter? *Dear Former Lover . . .* It didn't bear thinking about.

'If I were you I wouldn't give him another thought,' said Jonathan. He cut himself a fat wedge of Brie. 'Easier said than done, I know, but . . .' He flung himself back against the sofa and closed his eyes, humming along with the record. '*Mann und Weib, und Weib und Mann . . .* God, Mozart is sublime.'

Catherine thought of the letter she had received that morning. Sitting opposite Liz at breakfast she'd intercepted the look which had passed between her and Guy, as she slit open the envelope with the American postmark. Since the Meyers' departure, Liz's attitude towards her had been solicitous, almost apologetic, as if she felt responsible in some measure for the way things had turned out.

The writing was unfamiliar but the tone was not. *Dear Cathy,* she had read, *Just wanted to say Hi and send you our new address! We are all fine and the baby is well and putting on weight! I can't believe it's over two months since we left Edinburgh. We stopped over in London on the way home but the weather was terrible!* Catherine's eye skimmed a couple of paragraphs describing the journey. *Ithaca is a nice place,* the letter continued, *and we've met a lot of new people. Our house is rented from a senior professor who's on sabbatical in England so we don't have to worry about finding a home of our own until next year. Saul's hoping to get a faculty appointment before then, of course. He met his new supervisor for the first time a couple of days ago. Apparently, he was really impressed by Saul's thesis work so far and thinks it might end up as a book. My husband, the writer!* Another couple of paragraphs followed, describing the people they'd met and the parties they'd been to. Aaron's rate of growth and feeding habits. His resemblance to his father . . .

Catherine turned over the page, to find herself apostrophised. *Cathy, how are you? I often think of you and wonder how you're getting on* . . . It was the point in the letter when the heart of the matter is reached. The closing sentences. The valedictory remarks. It was like the moment at a party when the departing guests, awkwardly standing around in their coats, say the things they've been meaning to say all evening. *I'm sorry if you were hurt by some of the things I said, the last time we talked. But you must have known as well as I did that what happened with you and Saul could never have worked out. In his own way Saul's a very moral person, you know? As far as he knows* . . . This was it, Catherine thought, the point of the letter. . . *I know nothing about it. I haven't told him the truth. It seems to me neither of us is ready to face it just yet. We've got such a lot of things to work out – adjusting to the baby, Saul's work program – that I think the last thing we need is to question the foundation of our marriage.* So much for honesty, Catherine thought. A selective honesty, evidently.

Maybe one day you'll understand . . . Virginia went on, beginning a new page.

'Anything interesting?' said Liz brightly. In the loose fitting, earth-toned smocks and sweaters she had adopted since the confirmation of her pregnancy, she looked more than ever like a member of some nineteenth-century community of freethinkers specializing in plain living.

'Not really. Virginia sends her love.'

. . . *or maybe you do already. I guess we all had something to learn from the experience. You know, in spite of everything, I still think of you as my friend. Tell Liz and Guy and the others hello, won't you? With fondest thoughts, Virginia.*

At the bottom of the page, beneath Virginia's florid scrawl, was written *Love from Saul.*

Catherine stared at the words for a long time after she had finished reading the letter. Saul's precise, backward-sloping hand, standing out from the text by virtue of its spikiness, the mixture of awkwardness and pedantry suggested by the formation of its characters, touched her in a way the letter had not. She pictured the circumstances under which it had been written. Virginia casually pushing the finished page, with just space for a valediction, across the table to where he sat working. Blind to everything but the words on the page in front of him as, steadily, pedantically, he filled up page after page of notes. *Love from Saul*. Had he scribbled it in a moment of abstraction, irritated perhaps at being disturbed? Or was there an element of deliberation about the writing, suggesting he had reflected before putting pen to paper? Had he, perhaps, read what was in the letter? Virginia would hardly have been so careless as to permit it. It was impossible to tell. However hard she looked, she found herself unable to read between the lines.

Catherine received one further communication from her former lover. It was a few days into the New Year. She arrived back at the flat in London Street late one evening, at the close of the Christmas holidays. As she turned into Great King Street she saw the Gothic spire of St Stephen's church raising an admonitory finger in the waning light, a granite invocation of all that was the past. The tenements in London Street appeared deserted, with only a few of the windows lit, giving them more than ever the look of stage flats in a theatre which has gone dark. She climbed the stairs and let herself into the flat, which was cold and had a damp, unaired smell.

She lit a fire in the living room and began to sort through the pile of mail which had accumulated during her absence. Late Christmas cards. Circulars. Final demands. There was also a postcard. A picture of unfamiliar collegiate buildings. Red brick. Gothic arched windows. A prospect of green lawns. Ithaca, NY. She turned the card over and read what was written there.

> And that this place may thoroughly be thought
> True Paradise, I have the serpent brought.

There was no signature. Instead, in the bottom right-hand corner, the serpentine initial.

Catherine found the book, opened it at the appropriate place, read the verses referred to and closed the book, with the card inside marking the place. It was some years before, searching for something else entirely, she found it again.

To give up another person's love is a mild suicide.

(Wyndham Lewis, *Tarr*, 1928)

Tout, au monde, existe pour aboutir à un livre.

(Stephane Mallarmé,
Letter to Henri Cazalis, November 1864)